# A Purrfect
# Romance

Center Point
Large Print

**This Large Print Book carries the
Seal of Approval of N.A.V.H.**

# A Purrfect Romance

## J.M. BRONSTON

CENTER POINT LARGE PRINT
THORNDIKE, MAINE

This Center Point Large Print edition
is published in the year 2014 by arrangement with
Kensington Publishing Corp.

The text of this Large Print edition is unabridged.
In other aspects, this book may vary
from the original edition.
Printed in the United States of America
on permanent paper.
Set in 16-point Times New Roman type.

ISBN: 978-1-62899-205-2

Library of Congress Cataloging-in-Publication Data

Bronston, J. M.
  A Purrfect romance / J. M. Bronston. — Center Point Large Print
edition.
    pages cm.
  Summary: "Bridey Berrigan figures housesitting two cats in a
penthouse will give her the perfect opportunity to write her dream
cookbook, but the intriguing neighbor proves to be a distraction"
—Provided by publisher.
  ISBN 978-1-62899-205-2 (library binding : alk. paper)
  1. Housesitting—Fiction. 2. Food writing—Fiction.
  3. Cookbooks—Fiction. 4. Authorship—Fiction.
  5. Domestic fiction. 6. Large type books. I. Title.
PS3602.R64269P87 2014
813′.6—dc23
                                                        2014016068

# Acknowledgments

My thanks must begin with a most appreciative nod to a very special man, Damien Miano. It was Damien, who knows everyone, who set everything in motion. Without him, I would not have found Liza Fleissig and Ginger Harris-Dontzin and their amazing LizaRoyce Literary Agency. Liza is a treasure of energy and effective representation, and I cannot imagine my literary life without her. To my editor, John Scognamiglio, and to Rebecca Cremonese and the whole team at Kensington Books, I owe my most sincere and grateful thanks. An author dreams of the kind of care and attention I've received from them. With my deepest affection, I acknowledge two special friends from childhood—Harriet Harvey, who was present at the creation, and Sheila Kieran, who has been my role model in so many ways. And then there are The Six—Janet Asimov, Barbara Friedlich, Leslie Bennetts, Sandra Kitt, and Carrie Carmichael— wonderful, intelligent and creative women who have been a precious source of good professional advice, encouragement, and support. (In case the reader notices that I've named only five, I assure you, no one has been slighted; I am the sixth of The Six,) I also thank most warmly an old friend, Mary Santamarina, at the New York County

Surrogate's Court, who was an invaluable legal resource. To the many friends and associates who have encouraged and guided me along the way, no page is long enough to name you all and express my thanks as fully and as sincerely as you deserve. I have appreciated every word of affection, advice, and support you've given me.

But most of all, I acknowledge my three girls, Annie, Mary, and Margaret. Thank you for everything. You already know what you have given me.

# Prologue

The Last Will and Testament of Henrietta Lloyd Caswell Willey lay open on Douglas Braye's big cherry wood desk, and Doug Braye himself was glaring at it malevolently, his gray eyes narrowed under his bushy eyebrows. Even his hair, white and wiry like his bristling eyebrows, seemed charged with angry electricity. He tapped his pencil on the desktop in irritation. Behind him, from its place of honor on the paneled wall, the enormous portrait of his father, old Mason Braye, dead now these twenty years, looked down severely, seeming to join his son in an effort to find words adequate to express their combined displeasure.

Finally, having reached the limit of his exasperation, Douglas tossed the pencil onto the papers in front of him and leaned back in his chair.

"The woman must have been mad!"

Gerald Kinski said nothing. What could he say? He picked nervously at a tiny wisp of lint that rested on the lapel of his pin-striped suit. He fidgeted with his bow tie. He ran his hand over what was left of his thinning gray hair. He'd been dreading this meeting with the other senior partners ever since the news of Henrietta's death had reached him, and now he slumped deeper into the big leather chair. Maybe, with luck, he could disappear into it.

"And you, too, Gerry. What could you have been thinking? How could you let this happen?"

This from Art Kohler, the third man in the room. Even in good times, Art walked under a cloud of gloom and doom, and right now he was more than usually morose. He paced back and forth in front of the windows as he always did when things were going badly, with his shoulders hunched and his hands clasped tightly against his vest, where his ulcer was flaring dangerously.

"I thought it was a whim," Gerald said miserably. "I thought I could get her to change her mind in time."

He felt stupid even as he said it. No one ever got Mrs. Willey to change her mind; eighty-four years old, with a will like iron, like a force of nature, an act of God, a great cosmic power, and even more so ever since Neville's death twelve years earlier. He remembered how he'd tried, tactfully, to reason with her, and how she had risen imperiously from her chair.

"Just do it!" she had ordered as she sailed from the room.

Who'd have guessed, only three weeks later, she'd just suddenly fall dead like that? On a beautiful afternoon in early spring, a lovely day in April, just going out for her regular stroll down Park Avenue? Tom, the elevator operator, had opened the door for her, she'd gasped and rolled her eyes heavenward, whispered, "Oh, my dear

Neville," and there she was, dead as a doornail in poor old Tom's arms. The man was still in shock.

"Forty years this firm has been handling the Willey account," Douglas was saying, "and we've always given them solid, conservative representation. What would my father have said?" He gestured behind him to the portrait. "My father would have said this firm is now in the hands of idiots!"

Braye, Kohler and Kinski was one of New York's most conservative law firms; the three men were the sons of the firm's founders. They had devoted decades of their professional lives to carrying on the traditions their fathers had begun. And now Gerald Kinski, certainly old enough to have known better, had committed a lawyer's worst mistake. He had allowed an eccentric client's foolishness to outweigh his own good judgment.

"We'll be the laughingstock of the whole New York Bar," said Art, who stopped his pacing only long enough to throw his arms into the air. His eyes, always heavy lidded, underlined by deep, black, baggy circles, looked more miserable than ever, and he cast his gaze toward the ceiling as though he expected it to fall on them all.

"I know. I know."

Gerald Kinski felt the dignity of all his sixty years slipping away from him. Like a six-year-old who's been summoned to the principal's office, he was awash in shame and trepidation.

"And just wait till the papers get hold of this."

"I know. I know." Kinski was beginning to sound like a broken record.

"Stop sounding like a broken record, Gerry," Douglas said. He leaned forward on his desk, his elbows resting on either side of the offending papers, his fingertips pressed against his temples. "My God. Seventy million dollars and she's left all of it to a couple of goddamn cats."

He looked down at the paragraph and read aloud: " '—and being without surviving heirs and there being therefore no natural objects of my bounty, I hereby direct that the residue of my estate—' "

Here Douglas looked up from the paper and interrupted his reading to snarl at his squirming partner. "That's seventy million dollars, Gerry. Seventy goddamn million dollars."

He forced himself to calm down enough to go on reading. " '—the residue of my estate, including my apartment at Six Twelve Park Avenue and all its contents, shall be placed into a trust, the proceeds of which shall be used solely for the care and support of my beloved companions, Silk and Satin. I further direct that the said apartment together with its contents shall be maintained as their residence and that the said trust shall terminate only upon the demise of both of them, except that if there be issue of either of them, such trust shall continue in full force and effect for the benefit of such issue, in perpetuity—' "

Again, Douglas looked up from the paper as though he couldn't believe what he'd just read. "It's crazy," he said sharply.

"I know. I know."

"And what's this 'in perpetuity' crap? You know better than that! A first-year kid in law school knows better than that!"

Gerry shrugged helplessly. "I know," he said weakly. "But she insisted—"

Art Kohler stopped his pacing long enough to stare down to the sidewalk forty-three floors below. He apparently decided against jumping and instead dropped into one of the empty chairs.

"That fancy Park Avenue apartment," he moaned, "and all its contents—enough antiques to stock Sotheby's auction house. Eighteen rooms. Seven bathrooms. A wood-burning fireplace in every bedroom. And that kitchen! It's big enough to feed the whole Russian army. All for two goddamn cats. How could you, Gerry?"

"I know."

"Oh, stop saying that!" Douglas squared his shoulders and picked up his pencil. "We have to think. We have to do something."

He tapped for a while.

Then he said, "First of all, we have to get someone to live in that place, take care of those animals." He made some notes on a yellow pad.

"Post an ad somewhere, Gerry. Something discreet. Get us someone sensible, reliable.

11

Someone who won't give us any trouble. Someone who'll appreciate a chance to live rent-free in a dream apartment. I'll leave it up to you to handle the screening—but try not to screw it up, okay? Maybe we can keep the press away from this."

He dropped his head back into his hands and dug his fingers into his bristling hair.

"Oh, God!" he groaned. "My father must be spinning around in his urn."

## Chapter One

The traffic light changed, dozens of impatient cabs charged into motion—and Bridey Berrigan sprinted to the median strip, just a jump ahead of disaster. She should have been more careful, but on this particular morning she was too excited to watch the traffic. All her attention was on her new home, across the street at the corner of Sixty-Sixth and Park.

There it stood, tall and gleaming in the morning sunlight, a peaceful oasis in the midst of the city's rush. She checked the address spelled out in elegant lettering on the green canopy that stretched across the sidewalk from the glass-and-wrought-iron door all the way to the curb.

"Six Twelve Park Avenue," she whispered into the city's racket.

She looked once again at the slip of paper on which Mr. Kinski had written the address.

"Apartment Twelve A."

She counted the floors up to twelve, the penthouse level, and saw trees and shrubbery waving in the breeze, poking their newly green tops over the terrace railing, and Bridey, who couldn't help being nervous on this very important day, was reassured by the greenery in the sky. It seemed to be a happy omen, as was the morning sunlight that flashed brightly off the twelfth-floor windows.

The breeze caught at her hair and she raised a hand to smooth the thick, crinkly mass of curls that fell almost to her shoulders, holding it back from her forehead so that it formed a veritable halo of copper and gold around her remarkably fine-featured face. Her gesture unleashed flashes of sun-filled brilliance that danced happily around her head, adding to the shimmering, eager excitement in her golden-green eyes.

Mr. Kinski's words were still singing in her head.

"There's very little that will be required of you," he had said during their interview in his office, as he described the peculiar nature of the job. "Until the probate of the will is completed, nothing can be removed, so everything is being maintained exactly as it was before Mrs. Willey's death. There are eighteen rooms, a full cleaning staff and excellent building security. And the kitchen—well, I think you'll find it will exactly suit your special purposes. As you will see, it had originally been designed to accommodate the most elaborate social functions. So, all in all, this should be a very comfortable arrangement for you."

A comfortable arrangement indeed! *Perfect* was more like it.

"And then, of course," he had added, "there are the two cats."

Ah, yes. The two cats.

Silk and Satin. A pair of highly pedigreed Russian Blues from a single litter.

The ad had practically jumped at her off the screen.

> House sitter needed for indeterminate period. Must love cats.

She needed a place to stay. She loved cats. She answered the ad. Simple as that!

And now, as she waited for the light to change, she said to herself, "This is either the nuttiest thing I've ever got into or some good angel is watching over me. This could be the most fabulous piece of good luck, a heaven-sent chance to change my whole life."

Nutty or fabulous?

Sometimes Bridey couldn't tell the difference. Her style had always been a happy combination of sharp turns and quick energy, which often turned her adventures into scrapes and her scrapes into adventures. Her Grandma Berrigan, who had raised her, liked to say, "That child is all nuts and cherries."

At school, the sisters had put it a little differently.

"Bridey Berrigan!" they'd chuckle to each other in make-believe despair. "That one is definitely a fruitcake!"

The light changed again and she hurried across the street to number 612 where Max, the doorman, stood discreetly on guard, as he had every morning for more than twenty years. Max was impeccably sharp in his blue uniform and brass buttons, and as he opened the door for Bridey, the glass surfaces made his image dance in multiple reflections.

She gave him her name. He smiled politely.

"Yes, Miss Berrigan," he said. "Mr. Kinski has already arrived. He's waiting for you upstairs, in apartment Twelve A." He gestured toward the elevator and then watched her as she walked across the lobby. He gave high marks to the trim, lithe figure in the bright yellow outfit and summery heels.

For her part, Bridey was more aware of the beautiful dark wood paneling of the walls, the brass fixtures all polished to a high gloss, the unfamiliar click of her heels on the marble floor. She tried to feel comfortable in the elegant setting.

"Quite a change from old Mrs. Willey," Max said

to Sergei, the hall porter, who had just come on duty. They both turned to study her discreetly while she waited for the elevator. "Them's sure a couple of lucky kitties," Max added.

Sergei, who was still learning English, said only an enthusiastic, "For sure!"

A moment later, similar thoughts were in the head of Tom, the elevator operator. Poor Tom; he was the father of seven noisy children and his sanity depended on the daily, uneventful quiet of his job, and he still hadn't gotten over the shock of Mrs. Willey's startling demise. Out of the corner of his eye, he checked out the new resident as they rode up to the twelfth floor, and he definitely approved. He was reassured to see that this one appeared to be in full—and very attractive—good health.

"That's Twelve A, miss," he said as he opened the door, pointing to the door to the left.

There were only two apartments on the floor and the other door, marked 12B, was directly opposite, to her right. Between the two doors, a pier table against the wall held a vase with cut flowers, and a mirrored panel above the table reflected Tom's face behind her, smiling as the door closed.

To the right of the table, a brass umbrella stand held one very black, very conservative, very tightly rolled umbrella. Its handle was the old-fashioned kind, made of real bamboo stained a dark brown.

She glanced at the door to 12B, wondering about her neighbor.

Just one umbrella, she thought. And definitely not a female one. Judging by the severity, the extreme correctness of the umbrella's style, its owner must be really conservative. She imagined a gentleman of the old school, correct and unapproachable, aloof in his trim, perfectly tailored overcoat, maybe dove-gray gloves, striped pants and an understated, dark tie. In her fantasy, she dressed him in the clothes of a bygone time. He'd be about eighty, impeccable in his manners and very private, just the sort of man she'd expect to be living in this very old-money, very well-behaved building. But he'd remain aloof, of course; she'd learned by now that the inhabitants of this densely populated city valued their privacy.

*Well, that's all right,* she thought. *I'm here to work. I can't waste any time socializing.*

She gave the tangle of copper curls one last, nervous pat, smiled at her reflection in the mirror for encouragement, and rang the bell.

"She's perfect!"

Gerald was hoping to placate the partners, let them know he'd found the right person for the job.

"She loved the cats," he told them reassuringly, "and they took to her instantly."

He sat forward in the big leather chair, the very picture of optimism, eager to impart only good news. He refused to be put off by Art Kohler's customary pacing and air of certain disaster, or by Doug Braye's impatient tapping of his pencil on the desk blotter.

"She grew up in a big family, with lots of pets," he went on, trying to make up lost points with his partners, "in a small town somewhere upstate. You should have seen how those two cats just snuggled right up to her. First thing she walks in and just stands there looking around with her mouth open—well, you know how that place is, like a museum, with all those carpets and crystal and first editions. And that enormous living room with the sun pouring in through those big windows—and then Silk and Satin are there, nuzzling up around her ankles like she's their mommy or something. Jeez, I never saw anything like it. She was down on the floor with them in a minute—right there in the foyer—and they were all sniffing noses like they were saying how-do-you-do. They really did make a pretty picture, those two cats with their sleek gray coats and her with this head of red hair. Well, not red, really—"

Gerald seemed to get distracted momentarily, sidetracked down some mental lane. *If I were thirty years younger,* he was thinking, remembering the pale dusting of freckles across her short, delicate nose, making her seem very young and innocent—

"Gerry?" Doug brought him back. "You were saying, Gerry?"

"Oh, yeah. I was just remembering how nice she looked, real nice, you know? Playing with the cats, like a kid. Pretty girl she is, with all that red hair and big green eyes. Silk and Satin will be in good hands with her."

"Young and playful, huh?" Art Kohler was still looking for trouble. "Do you think she's reliable? There's a lot of valuable stuff in that place. Will she be careful, do you think? We have to be damned sure nothing happens to those two cats. Anything happens to those cats, we're in big trouble. You're sure she understands?"

"Oh, sure. I made it real clear—absolutely clear—the safety and prosperity of those two cats is her solemn responsibility."

"And you checked her out thoroughly?"

"Of course. And I'm satisfied she's okay. She's twenty-four and unattached. Her parents died in a car crash when she was just a kid, and she was brought up by her paternal grandmother and a mob of uncles and aunts and cousins. She has no family here in the city. She's been living with a girlfriend for the last few months."

"Where'd she go to school?"

"She graduated from the Culinary Institute at Hyde Park. Where, I might add, she took special honors as a pastry chef. I called the dean there and he gave her a first-rate recommendation, said she's totally steady, dedicated to her career. She's been working at the Cheval Vert for the last couple of years, but now, with this chance to live rent-free, she's quit her job and plans to work full-time on a special project—some kind of cookbook, I think. She's got enough saved to live on, buy her supplies, do her research, that sort of thing. She's really dedicated a hundred percent to this project and she needs a place where she can test her recipes. That big kitchen in the Willey apartment is absolutely a godsend for her. She was ecstatic when she saw it."

*Ecstatic* was hardly the word for it. She'd been impressed, of course, as Mr. Kinski led her through the vast apartment, through its many bedrooms, through the separate suites for Neville and Henrietta, through the library, the guest rooms, the servants' quarters, the laundry room, and the sewing room. But he had saved the best for last, and when he opened the swing doors into the huge, virtually professional kitchen, Bridey's mouth opened in a sudden, involuntary *o* and her eyes went wide.

*This is spooky,* she thought, looking round at the spotless chrome and white tile. The simple ad had said nothing about a kitchen, but the brief notice had jumped out at her as if it had her name on it. She'd taken a chance and now, like magic, a fabulous door to her future was opening, as though divine providence had taken an unexpected shine to her.

"Mr. Willey had been in the diplomatic service," the lawyer explained, "and he and his wife entertained on a very lavish scale. You've seen the dining room."

She was recovering from her first astonishment and, while Mr. Kinski kept talking, she proceeded to walk around the enormous workstation in the middle of the kitchen, trailing her hand lovingly along the impeccable countertop, touching appreciative fingers to the hanging pots and pans, the racks of exotic utensils suspended above the work surface, the drawers below containing every imaginable cooking aid.

"It's perfect," she whispered, more to herself than to him. "Just perfect."

"The dining room alone seats twenty," he added, "and the Willeys often had a hundred or more for cocktail parties and fund-raising affairs. Mrs. Willey was enthusiastic about good cooking, like yourself, and because her husband had been posted all over the world, she had developed considerable culinary experience. She was always collecting new recipes. If she had a guest from a foreign country, she'd take him—or his wife—into the kitchen to teach her chef the secrets of some new dish or exotic cooking technique. They might all wind up spending the evening in the kitchen with the cooks instead of in the living room trading small talk. Maybe that was the secret of her social success; guests had an interesting evening at the Willey parties and invitations were highly valued.

"Unfortunately," he added sadly, "that all changed when she became a widow. Her husband's death was very hard on her. She actually went through a severe personality change. She'd always been very high-strung and dramatic, and people put up with her sharp tongue because she was lively and amusing and gathered interesting people around her. But after Mr. Willey died, she turned reclusive and somewhat eccentric. Bad tempered, even. Eventually she drove away all her friends. There were no more parties, no more dinners, no more social life. This extraordinary kitchen," his hand gestured around the room, "this virtually professional setup, was reduced to providing only the simple meals she took by herself. She had no family, and she wound up, at the end, all alone in the world. So sad."

Mr. Kinski paused, remembering the white-haired, stiff-necked old woman, remembering how she'd glower at him during her visits to his office, remembering how immovable she was once she'd made up her mind about anything.

"However," he continued at last, "she kept everything in first-class condition, and I think you'll have everything you need here to do your work."

"Oh, yes," Bridey replied. "Everything. It couldn't be better."

She said a silent prayer for the long life and

continued good health and safety of the two beautiful cats.

"So, if everything is in order," Mr. Kinski said, "you can take over immediately."

He walked to a deep alcove at one end of the kitchen where, on a long table topped in butcher block, a bottle of red wine and two glasses waited.

"I've taken the liberty," he said, "of preparing for this moment. I opened it before you arrived so it would have a chance to breathe."

He poured out two glasses, handed one to her and lifted his in a toast.

"To the success of your book," he said.

She sniffed, swirled and sipped, approving the excellent Bordeaux. Then she lifted the glass again, in a toast of her own.

"To Silk and Satin," she said. "Long may they live."

# Chapter Two

"Tell me all about it!"

The excited voice on the telephone pierced the remnants of Bridey's dreams. She opened one eye just enough to see the clock next to her bed.

"Marge," she groaned, "it's not even seven o'clock."

"Yes, it is. Well, practically. And I couldn't wait another minute." Marge's voice was at its usual hypomanic pitch: enthusiastic, endearing, and always irresistible, like a small bell going *ding! ding! ding!* "Come on, Bridey, tell me all about it. Is it magnificent?"

Bridey lifted her head and looked around sleepily. Yes, the Queen Anne highboy was still there, between the tall windows that opened out to the terrace. And the thick, pale beige carpeting that contrasted so delicately with the soft rose of the walls. There was the mirrored dressing table, with its silver and crystal accessories, and opposite her bed was the enormous dressing room in which her small wardrobe now hung in modest simplicity. It hadn't all disappeared during the night. It was not all a figment of her dreams. She was really here, on Park Avenue, in the most stunning apartment she'd ever seen, like something out of *Architectural Digest*. She snuggled luxuriously into the lush bedding that surrounded her.

"Yes, Marge," she said dreamily. "It really is magnificent. When I get settled, you've got to come up and see it."

"I can't wait! And will you really be able to work on your book there?"

"Absolutely. The kitchen is unbelievable. It's huge and totally professional. I'll be starting this morning. First thing."

"Cool! That's so cool! I want to buy you breakfast, to celebrate. I won't keep you long. Just a quick cup of coffee."

"Well—"

"I promise I won't stand in the way of culinary progress, but I just have to hear all about it. Forty minutes. No more. I promise."

"Well, okay. As long as we make it really quick. Just give me a half hour to shower and dress. And feed the cats."

"Half an hour, at the deli on Lexington and Sixty-Fifth. I can't wait," Marge repeated. Her enthusiasm bubbled right through the phone. "Oh, Bridey, I can't get over how lucky you are!"

"I know. I'm the luckiest girl in New York."

She hung up. In the silence, she let those words resonate in her head.

*The luckiest girl in New York.*

She blinked a couple of times, stretched once —lazily—and smiled into the sunlight that streamed through the windows. Then, as though taking her energy from the brilliance of the day, she threw back the covers and sprang out of bed.

Silk and Satin were waiting for her outside the bedroom door, sniffing at her toes as she emerged and mewing hungrily around her bare feet, ready for their breakfast. They followed her impatiently through Henrietta's sitting room and down the hall to a room off the kitchen that had formerly been the servants' eating quarters but was now devoted entirely to the cats' care and comfort. Their bowls were on the floor, along with their beds—pink for Silk and blue for Satin, to match their embroidered collars. While they rubbed their heads against her ankles, Bridey washed out the bowls, dried them with a paper towel, and refilled them with fresh water and the special dry cat food that was custom mixed just for them and stored in a large wooden bin. Their litter boxes were in a small bathroom off the cats' dining room, and Bridey quickly cleaned them. These were her sole chores.

"Okay, you guys," she said. "You're on your own now."

She left them to their breakfast and went to the sumptuous bathroom, all marble and mirrors, where she quickly showered and dressed in jeans, T-shirt, and flip-flops. She went through the apartment to the cloakroom just off the parquet-floored, mirror-paneled foyer. Her denim jacket, her lightweight raincoat and her one good topcoat looked lonely hanging on one of the two long, empty rods on which hundreds of hangers waited for the masses of visitors who no longer came. She grabbed the jacket in one hand in case the day turned chilly, slung her large tote bag over her shoulder, and headed for the door.

"Be good, you two," she called to Silk and Satin as she left. "I'll bring you back a fish."

No empty promise. Later, as soon as she got organized, she'd be starting on her chapter entitled, *Fish: Fast and Mostly Fat-Free*, and her mind was already at work, mentally choosing and rejecting. Reluctantly, she'd have to omit one of her personal favorites, a Russian *coulibiac*.

*Even if I Americanized it,* she was thinking, *and substituted salmon for the eel, it's still too complicated for my purposes. All those layers of fish and rice and mushrooms and sliced egg and bean thread, wrapped up in* blinchiki *and pastry dough. Too elaborate for this book—but I'll definitely use it in the next one.* She made a mental note to include *coulibiac* in her next book, which was already in the planning stage. It would be titled, *The Guy Thing: For Men Only,* and it would be a collection of recipes for the man who needs to have one specialty dish, some elaborate concoction, his very own signature dish to dazzle a date with.

She opened the door, and her thoughts were instantly scattered.

A large black dog of the retriever persuasion, trailing his leash, filled much of the hall and began instantly to sniff inquisitively at her.

The dog's owner, at the door to 12B, paused as the lock responded to his key, and he turned to glare at Bridey. She caught a glimpse of wavy black hair, fierce black eyes, and a very correct dark business suit under a lightweight raincoat. That, and a distinctly military bearing.

"Scout! Come!"

The man spoke sharply—angrily, in fact—and the dog responded instantly to his master's command. They both disappeared without another word as the door closed abruptly behind them.

*Well, hel-lo,* she said to herself. *So that's my new neighbor.*

Her fantasy of a gracious, gray-haired old gentleman was embarrassingly silly in light of the man's brusque snub, and she had to revise the image drastically.

Drastically!

Subtract about fifty years, first of all. Though she'd been right about the conservative part. This man looked starchy enough to freeze a bear in its tracks.

And what was he so mad about? She certainly hadn't done anything to earn that glare. Talk about your rude New Yorkers! She could almost feel her spine stiffen against the man's apparent hostility.

But still, you'd have to give him points for dynamite good looks. Almost took her breath away. What a pity. That such coldness came in such a handsome package.

"Well," she said to Silk, who was trying to squirm through the door as Bridey poked a foot at her to make her get back into the apartment, "at least the dog was friendly."

Mackenzie Haven Brewster shut the door behind him and leaned back against it, his hand still on the knob.

"Jeez, Scout," he said to the dog, who was nuzzling his hand. "Did you get a look at her?"

He closed his eyes, but the image of her still radiated brilliantly in his head, like a burst of sunlight, fixed in glowing colors on his retinas.

"I think they've thrown us a curve."

The dog looked up at him inquiringly.

"They couldn't get some little old white-haired biddy to look after those damned cats?" his master said. "Or some out-of-work actor, some guy with wild hair and noisy friends. Oh, no. Leave it to those scheming lawyers to come up with someone who looks like that."

It had been only a glimpse as she'd opened the door, but it had been enough. He'd seen the pretty, open face, the flash of coppery red hair with the light behind it, filling it with sprinkles of gold. He'd seen the slim, curvy figure in simple, casual clothes, the cordial smile turned so innocently toward him.

He took a deep breath, shook his head as though to clear it and opened his eyes.

"Not to worry," he announced forcefully to Scout. "She's not my type."

He took a step away from the door and tossed his newspaper onto a chair.

"No, she's definitely not my type," he repeated insistently, as though to head off an argument.

Mack Brewster liked his women tall, glamorous, and elegant. And the more pampered the better.

Pampered and dependent. He liked women who expected to be protected by men.

He peeled off his coat and dumped it in a disorderly heap on the chair, on top of the newspaper, instead of hanging it up in its proper place in the closet.

Then he stood there for a long time, right there in the middle of his foyer, with Scout circling around him, trying to figure out what was going on. Mack was a man of careful habits. Even before his years in the Navy, he'd been taught to keep everything around him shipshape. His shoes were always polished to a high shine, his pants were creased just so, and he never tossed his clothes around.

Scout knew something was up.

Mack picked up the phone on the hall table.

"Gotta call Maudsley," he said to Scout. He started to punch in the numbers. "Gotta find out—"

He stopped and looked at his watch.

"Too early." He stopped punching. "I'll get him later, at the office."

"Well, you're looking snarly," Marge said as she caught up with Bridey, who was just entering the delicatessen.

"Oh, Marge. New Yorkers can be so hostile."

Bridey was still feeling the irritation of her neighbor's glowering snub.

"Tell me about it," Marge said flippantly. She slid over on the leatherette seat and piled up her bag, her coat, her Bloomie's shopping bag and her Coach laptop case, all in a disorderly stack next to her. She tossed her long dark hair away from her eyes and picked a breadstick out of the basket that was already set on the table. She took a nibble of it, mentally counting the calories as she nibbled. "What happened?"

"Nothing," Bridey said. "Nothing unusual, that is. Just another Manhattan moment." She pushed her tote bag into the corner of the booth and picked up the menu.

"You didn't get mugged or groped or anything, did you?" Marge said absently. She was concentrating on the menu, calculating fat grams and her daily allowance of carbs.

"Nothing like that. Just a neighbor with an attitude."

"Happens all the time," Marge said. "By now you should be used to it."

"I'll never get used to it, Marge. Back home in Warrentown, people were so different. If someone moved in next door, you brought over a plate of cookies. This guy looked at me like I stole his morning newspaper or something. Too bad, too, 'cause he was really cute."

"Oh?" Marge was suddenly all attention. She put down her menu. "A cute neighbor? What else? Married?"

"How should I know?" Bridey remembered there was only one umbrella in the stand. "I don't think so."

"Well, well, well." Marge licked her bright red lips like a cat contemplating a canary. "So tell me all. Is he tall?"

"Yes."

"And dark?"

"Yes." Bridey remembered those black eyes glaring so fiercely at her. "Yes. Black eyes. Black hair." Wavy, she thought. Wavy and thick, but cut close and conservative . . .

"And handsome?"

"Very."

"Age?"

"I'd say late twenties, maybe early thirties."

"More. More. What was he wearing?"

"Something very starchy. White shirt. Dark tie. Dark suit. Very conservative. And a raincoat. A Burberry."

"All belted up?"

"What's the difference?"

"Oh, it's very important how a man wears his raincoat. Tells a lot about him."

Bridey was surprised to realize she could see him perfectly. As though he'd been photographed inside her head.

"His coat was open. Like he'd just thrown it on." Funny, about that. Maybe he wasn't altogether 100 percent starchy. "Yes, open. Loose over his business suit." Actually, rather casual, she thought. "And he had a dog," she added.

"Now that's really important! What kind of dog?"

"A big black lab. Very big."

"And well-behaved, I bet."

"Oh, yes. The dog was a perfect gentleman. Friendly, you know, not overtrained. But not a nuisance, either. His name is Scout."

"Omigod!" Marge waved her hands delightedly in front of her face, tossing crumbs from her breadstick. "You even know the dog's name!"

"So what?"

"So what? Oh, Bridey Berrigan, you are such an innocent. A good-looking neighbor with a dog. What could be better? A dog is the perfect excuse to get to know the guy. You really are the luckiest thing." She used the breadstick to tick off the items of Bridey's good fortune against the tips of her sculpted fingernails. "A fabulous apartment free of charge, a perfect kitchen, a quiet place to do your cookbook, a couple of sweet cats, and a cute guy next door."

"Yeah. Well, 'cute' won't cut it if the guy's temper is bad. No girl needs that."

"So what was he so mad about?"

"Beats me."

"Listen, Bridey. Take it from me, as soon as the aroma from your kitchen wafts out . . . well, you never know. Don't they say, 'The quickest way to a man's heart . . .'"

"I don't know if this one has a heart, Marge. Anyway, he's not my type."

"Oh, you could tell that right away?"

"Sure. Pure stuffed shirt. Black shoes polished for inspection. Upright and uptight. No, not for me, Marge. And anyway, the last thing I need is distractions. Especially the romantic kind. I have to concentrate on cooking and writing. Nothing else. This is my big chance and I mean to take advantage of it. No time for men." She scanned the menu. "I'm starved," she said, changing the subject. "Let's order."

Their waiter had arrived, and reluctantly, Marge picked up her menu and glanced at it. As usual, she wanted something special, something that wasn't listed.

"Be a dear," she said to the waiter, "and bring me just one egg. Poached. And please ask the chef to put a little white vinegar in the poaching water, and tell him not to let the yolk get hard. And one piece of dry toast. No butter. Leave off the hash brown potatoes. And black coffee. Would you possibly have a mocha/hazelnut blend?"

The waiter—sixty years old and tired—had had just about enough of demanding princesses on perennial diets. He shook his head impatiently and Marge said brightly, "Oh, all right, then. Just regular coffee." She picked up the pepper shaker from the table and held it up for his inspection. "Do you have a pepper mill? I'd prefer to grind my own."

"Listen, lady," he growled, writing down her order on his pad, "you want the Waldorf, you're in the wrong place."

Marge didn't even get that he was irritated. She smiled sweetly at him and handed him the menu.

"Well, then," she said. "That'll be all. And thank you so much."

Bridey had long ago given up trying to get Marge to go easy on these special requests of hers. Marge Webster was a dear and had a heart as big as Colorado, but she couldn't understand that a state of panic was business as usual in a restaurant kitchen, and her special orders were a nuisance. Marge had been Bridey's best friend since junior high, and Bridey had long ago gotten used to her friend's idiosyncrasies.

Bridey gave the menu one last, fast look.

"I'm starting work on my fish chapter today," she said, "so I'm in a fish mood." She looked up at the waiter. "I'll have the smoked salmon. And coffee." She handed him her menu and he disappeared grumpily.

"So tell me all. Is it fabulous?" Marge leaned forward expectantly, her fingers locked and her eyes eager.

"Yes, Marge. It's fabulous. More rooms than I can count. A living room big enough for a tennis court, and a terrace with a garden outside the bedroom. Gorgeous furniture. Thick carpets, fine paintings, the smell of money all over the place.

The cats are darling. What more can I tell you?"

"You can tell me more about your neighbor. I smell a romance around the corner."

"Marge, I have fish on my mind, not romance. So let's just drop it, okay?"

"No, I won't just drop it." When Marge had her head fixed on something, she was like a loco- motive going full steam ahead. "Frankly, I think you need a man to take care of you."

"What!" Bridey was shocked. "I can't believe those words just came out of your mouth! From you, of all people. You should know me better."

"Oh, don't get me wrong. What I mean is, you need to find out how good it is to be cared for. I don't mean you should give up and be a doormat. I mean sharing, when two people care for each other. You know, take care of and care for. You've never had that. You deserve it. That's all I mean."

"I'm fine. Just fine. It's my work that will take care of me, and I'm lucky to have work I love. Any man I love, or who loves me, will have to get out of the way of that."

"Whoops! Sounds T-U-F-F! If I didn't know you better . . ."

"Well, you do know me better."

"Okay, okay. But I don't get why you're so stuck on all work and no play. I mean, a little extra- curricular fun is good for a girl's health. It's good for the complexion and it keeps the shine in her hair."

"My health is just fine. And right now, this work is a whole lot more important to me."

"I know. I know. But—"

"There's no *but,* Marge. For the last five years, I've been locked into heavy-duty kitchen work. Do you have any idea what that means? Do you have any idea what restaurant work is like? People think it's glamorous, but they're wrong. It's crazy hours and hauling hundred-pound sacks of potatoes. Lifting huge tubs of cake batter and pots of boiling soup. And you'd better not ask for help. Men think women aren't tough enough for professional cooking. And just look at my hands." She held them out for Marge to see. "You can't work in a kitchen eighteen hours a day and not get cuts and burns. Your skin gets rough. There's dough under your fingernails all the time. And if you think equality for women has come to the kitchen, forget about it. The guys do everything they can to mess you up. You've got cakes in the oven, they'll turn up the heat to five-fifty when you're not looking, or turn it off altogether. Just to hassle you. They call it fun, but it can get mean. Like, once I was assisting this famous French chef; he really hated women in his kitchen. He'd get into these huge rages, and once he came at me with this enormous knife."

"What happened?"

Bridey smiled, remembering the scene.

"Oh, he calmed down when he saw I was ready

to use my rolling pin on him. But," she went on more seriously, "I don't want to live like that, Marge. I love cooking, but I don't love the craziness. So I mean to earn my living by writing cookbooks. That way I can get away from the nutso stuff and still stay in the business. But I can't do it part-time, in my 'off hours.' A professional chef doesn't have 'off hours.' So this cat-sitting job is my big chance. It's like heaven just opened up and dropped it in my lap. Like the gods are saying, 'Okay, Bridey Berrigan, we'll give you everything you need, just this one time. Now let's see if you can do it!' Do you think I'm going to throw that away? Do you think I'm going to waste my time mooning over some guy just because he's good-looking, unattached and lives next door? This is the big opportunity of my life and I'm going to use it! So that's that. I don't want to hear any more about it. Now," she said as the waiter arrived with their food, "let's just eat our breakfast."

"Okay, okay."

They were both silent for a moment.

"But still," Marge pouted a little and toyed with her poached egg, pushing it around with the tines of her fork, "but still, I can't help thinking a little romance will help keep the creative juices flowing. You shouldn't just slam the door on it."

"All right." Bridey gobbled down her salmon and smiled reassuringly at her friend. "I won't slam the door."

Marge brightened up. "Good! I just don't want this big career move to turn you all dried-up and wispy."

"Don't worry. All I need is two years. Maybe one, if I'm lucky." She looked at her watch. "But right now, I've got to get moving."

She gulped down her coffee, ate the last mouthful on her plate, and signaled the waiter to bring the check.

"Okay, Julia Child," Marge said as she gathered her stuff together. "I give up. You go back to your palace on Park and do your fishy thing. I've got to get to the office, too. Deadlines to meet, fires to put out, editors to yell at. Can't get the magazine out without at least one nervous collapse per issue. But your assignment," she added as they stepped out of the deli into the sunshine of Lexington Avenue, "should you choose to accept it, is to have some more information about Mr. Next Door the next time I call you. Some romance in your life, my dear, is like salt on your steak: A generous sprinkle will improve the flavor."

She planted an air kiss somewhere near Bridey's ear and was off to hail a cab.

"Don't call early," Bridey called after her. "I'll be at the fish stalls before dawn."

"Whatever." Marge leaned out of the window as the cab took off down Lexington. "But remember, think romance!"

"I'm thinking fish!" Bridey called, but Marge's

cab was by now indistinguishable from all the others.

"Fish," she repeated to herself as she stopped in at the fish store near Sixty-Sixth Street to pick up a treat for Silk and Satin. "I have only fish on my mind."

Only fish.

Well, not quite. The mental photograph of the man in the Burberry raincoat kept turning its intriguing black eyes on her, challenging her mysteriously from across the hall.

Why on earth had he glared at her like that? He had nothing at all to do with her. And she had to concentrate on the work ahead of her. No time to be getting involved with a stuffed shirt, no matter how cute he was. Though he was awfully good-looking.

*Enough of this!* she told herself. *Forget about him.*

She took a deep breath and bought a pound of flounder.

# Chapter Three

"Hey, you guys! Guess what I brought for your dinner."

Silk and Satin were already at the door as she entered the apartment, and they circled around her feet as she went into the kitchen.

"A nice, fresh flounder," she said, lifting the package out of her tote bag.

They meowed at her.

"For dinner, I said. Not now." She put the package into the fridge. "If you think I'm going to let you turn into a couple of fat cats, you're meowing up the wrong cat sitter." She made shooing motions at them. "Take off, you two. Go find something else to do."

Silk and Satin got the message. They retreated into the living room, where Satin quickly appropriated a bright patch of sunshine that filled the corner of the sofa. He arched himself once gloriously, seeming to say, "I win!" and then curled himself up into a languid ball, his blue-gray coat making an exquisite contrast with the pale yellow Italian silk of the upholstery.

Silk disdained his victory and, as though she for one didn't care, sauntered to the French window, which was slightly ajar, opening onto the railed balcony outside. She slipped through the narrow space and took up a position along the edge of the balcony, next to a pot of geraniums, and stretched herself out comfortably.

Actually, Silk preferred this place. It was comfortable for birdwatching and sun-warmed snoozing when the weather was mild. From here she could watch the fascinating, swiftly moving life that flowed far beneath her luxurious quarters. The busy traffic below intrigued her, and she often passed long hours filled with primeval cat curiosity, her green eyes slitted and provocative, fantasizing about life out there in the teeming city. She longed to go exploring in the busy streets below and thrilled herself by imagining exciting adventures and intriguing feline encounters, dreaming of dark alleys and new vistas . . .

Catlike, both Silk and Satin were soon sound asleep, and for the next few hours they lolled in cat oblivion, only coming awake every now and then to change positions or to make a companionable visit to Bridey. With typically feline sensitivity, they had caught on that something exciting had come into their previously predictable world, and they interrupted their snoozes occasionally in order to check out Bridey's progress in the kitchen.

Two possessions Bridey prized above all others.

The first was the medal on the broad blue ribbon that had been placed around her neck at her graduation from the Culinary Institute. It signified that, after years of attending classes, slaving over hot stoves, wearing a shapeless white jacket and dorky checkered pants and being snarled at by men who actually believed that women didn't belong in the kitchen—professional kitchens, that is—she was finally, really a fully credentialed, certified, bona fide, professional chef. She was immensely proud of her blue ribbon, and she vowed it would always have a prominent place in any kitchen in which she worked. She took it from its case, chose a hook over the workstation in the center of the kitchen and hung the medal there, where it could watch over her, like a good-luck charm.

But her other treasure was even more precious than her blue ribbon. She took from her suitcase a plain wooden box, about the size of a loaf pan, with brass hinges and a brass clasp long discolored by age and use. The box had been stained a dark brown and on its top, etched there long ago by loving hands, was the name Merrill. Bridey ran her fingertips over the surface for luck, and then opened the box to see once again the contents she knew so well.

More than 150 years had passed since Jane Hamilton Merrill, Bridey's great-grandmother's grandmother, had presented this box to her only daughter, Eleanor, on the evening before her wedding day. Eleanor, in turn, had given it to her daughter, Catherine, and so the Merrill Box, as Bridey called it, had eventually come down to her mother, Mary Berrigan. When Mary Berrigan died, it had been given to Bridey. The box contained Jane Merrill's favorite recipes and household hints, together with those cautionary words that old-fashioned mothers used to pass on to their daughters on their wedding day. Each bride in turn had added new items as she discovered—or invented—her own domestic and culinary secrets, the private techniques that became part of a time-honored family inheritance. The women of that line were all gifted cooks, and as each new bride in each generation added the treasures of her own kitchen, the collection grew into an invaluable trove of cooking and domestic lore, covering almost two centuries.

The beautiful old box was all the legacy Bridey had from her mother and she truly believed—from deep in that place where each of us truly believes in magic—that Mary Berrigan and all the Merrill women before her were smiling down on her because now, at last, in Bridey's time, the ancestral family skill could be practiced as an honored profession. The opportunity that had been denied to them was now realized in their descendant. She hadn't said so to Marge, but her deepest motivation in choosing to write cook-books was not only to practice her skill but to preserve and communicate it.

She carried the Merrill Box into the kitchen and placed it in the center of the counter, where it would remain until she'd found exactly the right spot for it.

And now she could begin her work.

First, she examined her laboratory, taking careful stock of everything it contained.

"You could run a full-scale restaurant out of this place," she whispered to herself, touching in turn each of the copper sautoirs, the fish poachers and steamers, the stockpots and the crêpe pans. There was an immaculate six-burner stove with high-temperature salamander above, and even an institutional-size Hobart mixer. Obviously, the legendary parties that had once made Henrietta Willey famous as a social force had been backed up by a heavy-duty kitchen.

*If I can't create a first-rate cookbook here,* she said to herself, *I won't deserve to have been voted most likely to make Master Chef.* But instantly, the audacity of even thinking of such success scared her, and she put it quickly aside. *One thing at a time,* she reminded herself. *Today is just for getting started.*

So she spent the morning unpacking the boxes that had been delivered the previous afternoon, the equipment that had cost almost every penny of her savings. She chose the table in the alcove for her desk and by noon had finished setting up her computer and printer, her stacks of notebooks, her laptop, her digital camera, her files of recipes and correspondence. Her collection of cookbooks found a home along the deep windowsill that surrounded the alcove, along with folders of food photos.

And then came the most important tool of all: her treasured Merrill Box. She held it in her hands reverently and whispered to it, as though she was casting a spell, "Please, all you Merrill women who came before me, help me in my work and make everything turn out well."

She placed it in the center of the windowsill, where the afternoon sun would fall softly on it every day.

Then, with trembling fingers, Bridey set her work plan on the only remaining open space on her desk. She opened it to her proposed table of contents, took a deep breath and found that her heart was pounding and her hands were shaking.

*Oh, God,* she thought. It burst upon her like a lightning strike: the moment she'd prepared for, the dream that had had its birth when she was still little, when she used to bake miniature pies and biscuits and cakes at her grandmother's side. It was staring her right in the face. She, Bridget Margaret Berrigan, was about to make her own contribution to her chosen profession.

"I'm so scared," she whispered into the silent room.

The enormity of what she'd done washed over her like a bath of pure, cold terror.

She'd burned all her bridges. Leaped off a cliff, sailed off the edge of the earth, closed all the doors behind her, whatever. She'd quit her job, used up all her savings and committed herself to this daunting task. Now she had to flap her wings as hard as she could and hope to fly.

She felt as though a flock of horrible demons had suddenly attacked her, appearing from nowhere, out of the corners of her imagination. She needed to catch her breath.

So she brewed a pot of coffee.

And while the water dripped through the grounds, she remembered what Marge had said.

Protection? Did she really need someone to protect her? The memory of the man next door swam through her thoughts, and she wondered why. If anything, he seemed to be breathing dragon fire rather than riding up like a knight in white armor. Not a good candidate if a girl was looking for protection.

And protection from what? From doing what she loved most in the whole world? From doing the very thing she was really good at? From standing on her own two feet? Marge, of all people, should understand. Marge, the most independent and self-reliant of people.

No.

She slapped a dish towel onto the countertop.

Hah! Protection, indeed.

No!

*I'll be okay!*

*I'll have to be okay!*

She squared her shoulders. She filled a mug with the brewed coffee. She paced around *her* kitchen, blowing on the steaming coffee to cool it, and as she did, the demons began to slink sullenly back into their corners. Her terrors settled down and her fears disappeared in the excitement of the task ahead of her. There was no place left to go but forward, and soon she was hard at work.

Hours passed and the sun was low over New Jersey, the last rays lighting up the tops of the buildings along Central Park West, and Silk and Satin came into the kitchen to tell Bridey it was dinner time.

"Oh?" she said, glancing at her watch, surprised at how the hours had disappeared. "Oh? Hungry, are you? In the mood for a little fish flake, are you? Okay, kids. Coming right up!"

In moments, she had poached the flounder in milk, flaked it into their bowls and, while they ate, changed their water. They were licking themselves clean by the time she had her own dinner ready: a sliced tomato and a boiled egg, some crackers, a glass of milk and a banana. While she ate, she looked over what she'd accomplished. Her work-station was covered with fish recipes. Her flash drive contained her introduction to the fish chapter. Her head was filled with updated ideas for the purchase, preparation and presentation of fish.

All she needed now was the fish.

She made a quick call to Charlie Wu, her old buddy from her days at the Culinary Institute. Charlie had his own restaurant now, just off Grand Street in Chinatown, and when Charlie needed fish, he didn't travel all the way up to the relocated Fulton Fish Market in the Bronx, where the big commercial suppliers now brought their catch. Charlie had his own sources, independent fishermen who continued to bring their fish directly to the old wharfs along the East River, down near the tip of Manhattan. Before dawn, under the shadow of the Brooklyn Bridge, only a few minutes away, he could meet up with them in the wee hours and get the freshest catch, with no middlemen, and catch up on the latest gossip. There'd be the rapid transactions, the unloading in the dark, the hustle and quick transfer into his van, and Charlie would leave with whatever he needed for the day.

"Sure," Charlie said. "Be glad to help out. Meet me dockside at four. We'll get you whatever you need. Might be chilly that hour of the morning. Bring a sweater."

"Thanks a bunch, Charlie. You're the best."

"You betcha." Charlie's smile was apparent right through the telephone. "Just be sure to mention me in your book."

"Of course. I'll give the restaurant a plug, too."

Bridey began her preparations. She set her big canvas tote bag next to the door.

"Dockside," she announced to Silk, who had come to inquire. "Before dawn."

From the cloakroom, she took a pair of waterproof boots and put them into the bottom of the bag. On top of that she added a sweater.

"It may be cold and wet," she said to Silk.

And a small, collapsible umbrella.

"You never know."

Then she went into the kitchen to get her laptop.

And as for Silk? What was Silk doing?

Silk was contemplating adventure. She knew something was up; she could feel exhilaration in the air.

She circled around the bag that stood next to the door, her tail tip twitching. She sniffed at the bag. It still carried the scent of the flounder that had been that night's dinner. She sniffed again and decided to follow her nose. What the hell! She had spent too many afternoons curled up on the outside balcony, observing the passing scene, wishing she could get out to explore. With the arrival of this new person in the apartment, she felt change in the air. Here, at last, was her chance.

She jumped into the bag and burrowed down into the soft sweater.

In the meantime, Bridey gathered up her note-pad, a pair of warm gloves, her shopping list, and her wallet. She took them to the waiting bag and dropped them in, not noticing that they landed on Silk's curled-up form.

Silk didn't complain; the extra items provided her with good stowaway cover.

Chefs are used to crazy hours. Four a.m., four p.m., it makes no difference in their workday. Bridey set her alarm for 3:45 and went to the bed-

50

room to grab a few hours' sleep. And Silk used those hours to do the same. When Bridey's alarm went off, she washed, dressed and scooped up the heavy bag, unaware that it contained a secret cargo.

Somewhere deep in Silk's primal memory there had been a dark ride like this, wrapped in something soft and thick, traveling rapidly over distance. Her neck fur bristled in excitement and anticipation, her adrenaline was flowing. Adventure was upon her.

Her inbuilt time sense knew it was night, the time for cats to prowl, but the bag in which she was being carried was still in motion. It jolted back and forth, start and stop and then start again, over and over, before finally being yanked up and hoisted out into the night air. Almost instantly, Silk was surrounded by noise and bustle and, oh, sweetest of all, the heavy scent, omnipresent, of fish. Fish enough for a lifetime of dinners. Let that stay-at-home, Satin, sleep in his comfy bed. She, Silk, was out in the real world. Oh, what stories she would bring home.

The bag came finally to rest, set down on cold concrete. Cautiously, she rose from her concealment, let an exploratory eye look over its top, saw Bridey's legs next to her, saw Bridey talking to someone, a mountain of cod between them, hands gesticulating, arms waving. This was her chance; no one was looking down at Bridey's bag. Silk took the opportunity. She slipped quietly out of the bag and in a moment had disappeared, like a gray shadow, into adventure land, where she was quickly engulfed by wondrous aromas, a mix of salt and fish, with quiet, urgent voices filtering through the dark night.

Some cat radar must have announced her presence: a new cat on the wharf! The regulars were there in a moment, checking her out, making their advances, inviting her to come and play. But Silk was true to her breeding; only the best would do. She ignored the scruffy toms, the ill-bred, whining, gossipy tabbies, the scroungers, the loafers, the adolescent, belligerent punks.

Yards away, curled up on the pilings, grooming himself luxuriously, a sleek black cat looked up from his splayed-out paws, and his eyes met Silk's. Some cat message passed between them. She stayed where she was, ignoring the presence of the others, and waited. Nightwatch—for that was the name given to him by the crew of the trawler on which he ferried nightly down from Nantucket— dropped silently down from the piling. He approached her, they made their introductions, and in a moment Silk had accepted his invitation. Together, they disappeared into the dark.

Meanwhile, Bridey was buying fish. An hour passed. From the handful of ships cleated up at the dock, thanks to a friendly introduction by Charlie, she selected cod, flounder and swordfish, twenty pounds in all, enough for her first round of recipes. Only the freshest. Only the best. She was satisfied. The first light of morning was beginning to turn the Brooklyn Bridge into a ghostly shadow riding over the shimmer of the East River. The sun would soon be up. It was time to go home. She packed the wrapped-up fish into her bag, surrounding it with layers of newspaper to keep it insulated and cool until she got it home.

As she bent over to pick up her bag, she chanced to look up.

And saw Silk.

"Omigod!" whispered Bridey.

The little stowaway looked sleeker than ever, with a kind of self-satisfied roll to her stride as she appeared out of the shadows, heading directly for Bridey, like baby to mama, as if she knew it was time to go home and she knew exactly how to get there. The tote bag was her means of transport and she was ready to hop in. Which she did, settling herself comfortably on top of the wrapped-up fish and looking pretty pleased with herself.

"Omigod!"

Bridey was aghast. This beautiful, sleek, refined animal, this uptown tourist making an unauthorized visit to the seaport, this totally out-of-place pedigreed puss, could be no other than the $70-million heiress that she, Bridey, was supposed to be caring for. The pink collar around Silk's neck was the confirmation. It was handmade, unique, and it had her name embroidered on it. This was no mistaken identity.

If Mr. Kinski found out! If *anyone* found out!

Omigod.

She whipped out the sweater and quickly plopped it down on top of the errant animal, stuffing the edges down the sides of the bag and darting her eyes around to see if she was being observed while trying to look casual and hoping it was dark enough and that the fishermen were too busy with their work to notice the disaster that was going on in their midst.

With one hand pushing down on Silk's protesting head, she got herself quickly to the street, lifting her hand from the bag only long enough to hail a cab, and never again moving it all the way home while keeping up a whispered scolding, with herself and the incorrigible cat as alternating targets of her frantic harangue. The cabdriver, who'd seen and heard everything during his years of hacking on the city streets, paid no attention.

"How could you? Oh, Silk, how could you? You could have gotten me into so much trouble! How could I explain if you'd gotten lost? If you hadn't shown up right there, at the very last moment, I'd never have known. I'd never have guessed where to look for you. Who would have thought you'd stow away in my bag?

"And oh, Bridey!" Now she began beating up on herself. "What would you say if she'd disappeared? 'Sorry, Mr. Kinski. I lost your cat. I know I'm supposed to be a responsible, grown-up woman, but you might as well have left Silk and Satin in the care of a chimpanzee!'"

Then again at Silk. "Who knows what could have happened to you? You could have gotten run over! You could have been attacked by stray dogs! You could have been kidnapped! You could have fallen in with the wrong crowd and—" The possibilities seemed endless, and her panic escalated drastically. "All my plans could have been ruined. Oh, Bridey, stupid, stupid, careless, dumb, dumb . . ."

By the time the cab pulled up to 612, she was a wreck. Theo, the night doorman, got no greeting at all from her as she passed him, for she was in no mood to be seen by anyone who knew her.

"Good morning, Miss Berrigan," he said to her back as she swept hurriedly by.

Oh, if only she could be invisible.

But there, just ahead of her, someone was waiting at the elevator. His back was toward her, and he was resting one hand against the wall, with his head drooped forward, as though it had been a long night and he couldn't wait to reach his bed. She recognized that Burberry instantly.

*Oh, rats!* she thought.

*Why did this have to happen now?*

*Why him, of all people?*

*And what was he doing coming in at this hour?*

He turned his head toward her just as Sandor, the night operator, opened the elevator door. He straightened up, pulling himself together in the presence of an observing human being. He said nothing, but his face wore a very small, preoccupied smile, as though something funny was going on in his head. His Burberry coat was unbelted and unbuttoned, and Bridey saw he was wearing a tuxedo. His black bow tie was uncharacteristically askew, his black hair was a bit disheveled, his black eyes looked privately mirthful, and there was lipstick on the edge of his collar. If Bridey hadn't been in such a distracted state, it would have registered more clearly that her neighbor's stuffed-shirt demeanor had slipped considerably; he actually looked quite human.

But she was too distracted. She was struggling to keep Silk under wraps, and to look as though it wasn't odd that the sweatery contents of her bag kept bobbing about. Her neighbor's smile broadened, a little crookedly. He was watching her in slightly tipsy amusement.

Sandor made light conversation while they ascended. "Looks like we're going to have a good day," he said. "Lots of sun. No rain predicted. Good day for your run, Mr. Brewster."

*Nice-looking couple, those two,* he was thinking. *They should get together.*

And he wondered why the pretty young lady was so stiffly silent, so rigidly preoccupied. The grapevine was already heavy with speculation about the twelfth floor. All the staff knew about old Mrs. Willey's bizarre legacy, they all knew what Mackenzie Brewster was up to, and they were making guesses as to the future of the two cats. There was even a staff pool betting on Mr. Brewster's next move.

His shift was almost over and when Tom came on, Sandor would have some new material to feed into the gossip mill.

"Have a good day, Miss Berrigan," he said as they got out at the twelfth floor. "And you, too, Mr. Brewster."

The door closed, and Bridey and her neighbor were alone in the little vestibule.

*I don't dare take my hand away from this bag. How do I get to my key without him catching on?*

On the floor in front of each door lay the morning newspaper, delivered only minutes before. Her neighbor dug into his pocket for his key and bent a little unsteadily to pick up his *New York Times*. He stood up and saw that Bridey was still standing in front of her own door. She was trying to look nonchalant, making no move to open her door, making no move to pick up her paper, making no move to do anything at all. In his slightly woozy condition, it seemed to him only moderately puzzling. With a broad gesture, an exaggeratedly chivalrous flourish, he picked up the paper that lay in front of the door to 12A and presented it to her.

"Allow me, madam," he said, and bowed his head slightly. There was still that little half smile on his face. She couldn't tell if he was being sarcastic or polite, but she was too panicky to care.

*Oh, please,* she prayed silently, *don't let him see what's in my bag.*

In her effort to be cool, Bridey's stance remained awkward, with one hand planted stiffly on top of her unruly cargo and the other holding the straps tightly at her shoulder, trying, with her elbow, to keep the bag close to her body. She allowed a couple of fingers to let go of the strap. He placed the paper in their weak grasp. The corner of her mouth twitched nervously into a tiny response, followed by a silly sound that wasn't yes, no, or thank you.

He raised one eyebrow, gave her—and her bag—a brief, quizzical look and opened his own door. The muzzle of the black dog appeared instantly, snuffling and eager for his master.

"Hey, there, old buddy," he said. "Good to be home at last. Did you miss me?" The door closed behind him.

Bridey relaxed. She leaned her head back against the wall, took one very deep breath and let it out slowly. At last it was safe to let go of her prisoner.

But Silk was in a perverse mood, and now that Bridey's hand was no longer pressing her down under the sweater, she lost all interest in pushing back. She merely raised her lovely though slightly mussed head and peered quietly over the top of the bag, while Bridey found her key, got the door open and got her whole disorderly baggage into the apartment.

Silk immediately ran off to tell Satin about her night on the town and Bridey sank, like a bundle of exhausted nerve ends, into the nearest chair.

"Oh, boy!" she whispered to the silent room. "Oh, boy, am I in trouble."

In the silence it seemed to her the pounding of her heart could be heard ten feet away. She listened to it for a while.

*That stuffed shirt in a Burberry raincoat.*

*He saw . . . he must have seen . . . I saw that he saw . . .*

She remembered his little smile as she'd tried to keep Silk quiet in the tote bag.

Still, why would he tell anyone? It was nothing to him. And if no one found out . . . and after all there had been no harm done, had there?

She was making herself calm down.

"Things to do," she said to the empty room. "Gotta get to work."

She remembered the twenty pounds of fish in her bag.

"Things to do," she repeated.

59

She got out of the chair and carried the bag to the kitchen. As she put the package into the fridge, she steadied her hand, leaning against the top.

"Maybe I'm not really in trouble," she said to herself.

And behind the door of 12B, Mack Brewster was in his bedroom, peeling off his fancy duds.

"Well, well, well," he said to Scout. "Looks like our pretty new neighbor had a little adventure of her own tonight." He sat on the edge of his bed, one patent-leather dress shoe in his hand. "What do you think, Scout? Is mum the word? Or should we spill the beans?"

Scout licked his hand enthusiastically and Mack added with a laugh, "Well, okay. I really ought to turn her in, but I couldn't treat a lady in distress that way."

He rubbed Scout's black head.

"I guess we can keep her secret for a while, anyway."

# Chapter Four

A week passed, and there were no repercussions, no outraged call from Gerald Kinski, no accusations of inexcusable incompetence and unforgivable neglect, no order to "get out, bag and baggage!" Though she couldn't forget her neighbor's presence, just the other side of the wall, there were no more chance encounters, and gradually she forgot her fear that she might unexpectedly run into him. As always, Bridey fought off anxiety by concentrating harder on her work, and by the end of the week, she had recovered her sense of security and her customary optimism. Her big scare had been only that, a big scare and nothing more. All would be well. Life was good.

The first draft of the fish chapter was done and, on this lovely Sunday morning, she was eager to begin work on *Breads and Rolls*. She'd been up early, proofing yeast and kneading dough and, while her first batches were rising, she decided it was time to allow herself a little rest from her labors. She washed up, carefully scrubbed out the dough from under her fingernails, pulled on a pair of tiny red running shorts, knotted up an over-sized T-shirt at her midriff, pulled her hair back with a bright red ribbon and headed out for a run through the park.

Central Park was in a spring mood, wearing its new, pale green foliage, just burst from the bud. Bright flower patches made good scampering grounds for bushy-tailed squirrels, and every-where—on the vast stretches of green grass and in the playgrounds and along the bench-lined walks—little ones played while their mommies, daddies and nannies gossiped with one another or read their newspapers. Streams of cyclists and inline skaters weaved along the paths, baseball players formed up their games on the ball fields and all New York was enjoying the lovely weather.

After a half-hour's run through the park, Bridey was breathing hard and glowing. It had been a week of worrying, but she was able now, at last, to feel carefree. She rewarded herself with a Popsicle from a vendor's cart and climbed up on an outcropping of rock. From there she could park herself for a while and watch the action on the Sheep Meadow—the pick-up games of smash ball, the dogs chasing Frisbees, the pigeons strutting about in the grass. The warm sunlight glistened off her damp shoulders and arms. It filled her hair with sprinkles of gold and heightened the sweet dusting of freckles that danced across her nose. In her little running shorts and floppy T-shirt, licking her Popsicle, she looked about ten years old.

She was totally unaware that for the last ten minutes her next-door neighbor had been watching her closely.

Mack Brewster was also out for a run that morning, with Scout loping along next to him, and when he glimpsed the halo of red and gold bobbing along ahead of him, he slowed down, not trusting his eyes.

For several days now, ever since their early-morning elevator encounter, he'd found himself unaccountably imagining he saw his pretty new neighbor. Again and again, everywhere he went, some bit of curly red-haired brilliance, some flash of a lithe young form would catch his eye, some girl going into a restaurant or waiting for a bus as he passed by in a cab, or just turning a midtown corner, or partly concealed in an after-theater crowd. He couldn't understand this obsessive phantom spotting, and he told himself it must be because she represented a seriously awkward snag in his plans. But would that account for the leap of eagerness that thumped in his chest every time he thought he saw her? Would that explain why every flash of coppery hair, disappearing in the crowd, made him want to follow after?

But the thumping was at top volume and he knew that this time he wasn't imagining anything. With Scout running beside him, he dropped into a slow jog, waiting for a chance to check her out, and when she stopped to catch her breath he stopped, too, sitting down on the grass about twenty feet behind her, pretending to be just another resting runner, hoping to blend into the great anonymous mass of Sunday recreationists. He rested his arms on his upraised knees and kept his head down so she wouldn't recognize him, allowing himself only a sideways observation of her from behind his unkempt, sweat-dampened hair. He watched as she bought her Popsicle and climbed to the top of the rock, where the sun lit her up like a spotlight, and he used the moment to enjoy his first good, slow look at her.

What he saw was a vibrant, healthy girl, with long, slim arms and legs, a trim torso, a graceful carriage and an unruly topping of sun-filled, red-and-gold hair.

"She looks like a kid," he whispered to Scout. "Like an innocent kid."

His heart bumped around in his chest, doing battle with his cool, disciplined, rational self. His head was telling him to avoid her, to remember that this temporary new neighbor of his, this breezy, sassy, sprite of a girl—not his type at all—stood in the way of his plans, his debt of honor. His mission, almost accomplished now.

But he should have known. Things had been going too smoothly. Just when things were coming together for him, thanks to Mrs. Willey's death, it seemed that the Fates, those unpredictable, cosmic tricksters, had slipped this unexpected ingredient into the mix. They'd playfully tossed him a confusing, distracting, green-eyed flash of sunlight.

How different she was from the usual New York sophisticates, the tough-talking colleagues who high-heeled their brash way through his offices, the mink-draped, perfumed heiresses who were usually on his arm in nightclubs and at charity events, the trust-fund babies he'd been set up with ever since his prep-school days, the potential trophy wives he'd been programmed to end up with and had been dutifully squiring around town ever since he'd grown into the age of eligibility. He'd assumed one of them would turn out to be the "right one." He was still waiting for that right one to click into place.

His better judgment was telling him to avoid this girl. But some other totally unfamiliar instinct was sending him a different message.

*Don't let her get away,* it was telling him.

"Go over to her, Scout," he whispered to his running companion, "and just sort of say hello."

Scout was nothing if not obedient and he promptly loped over to Bridey's rock, climbed it and planted himself next to her, reaching out an inquisitive nose toward her Popsicle.

Which gave Mack an excuse to follow right behind him.

"Hey, there, Scout!" His voice registered the irritation of an owner whose dog is being obstreperous. "Stop bothering the lady!"

Bridey looked up and saw a dark figure silhouetted against the bright sun, standing above her, tall and gleaming against the background of high-rising skyscrapers that sparkled beyond the rim of Central Park's massed trees.

"It's okay. He's not bothering me," she said, holding the Popsicle away from Scout's eager face. She shaded her eyes against the sun's glare to see the man's face. "Oh," she said, genuinely startled. "It's you."

And, pretending to be completely surprised, Mack repeated her words.

"Oh," he said, "it's you!"

"I guess it is," she said, disconcerted. All her recovered good spirits began to go shaky again. Just what she'd feared. Of all the people in the world, this neighbor of hers, this "cute guy next door," could make real trouble for her if he decided to tell what he'd seen that early morning, trying to sneak Silk back into the building.

"I didn't expect to see you here," Mack said.

"I didn't expect to see you here."

Still shading her eyes against the sun, she braced herself and took a good look at him, trying to figure out if she was in any danger. But this time, to her surprise, he was actually looking friendly. Maybe she could lighten up a little. After all, he didn't exactly have fangs or wear the mark of the beast on his handsome forehead.

And there was something else: Marge would be hungry for a report.

She decided to check him out quickly while he remained standing above her, backlighted by the sun. For Marge's sake, of course.

*Good body!*

She noted the sharp muscle definition of his arms and legs, the abdomen flat under his black running shorts and gray sweatshirt. He obviously worked out regularly. She also noted wryly that he some-how managed to keep that starchy air of solemn propriety even when he was shiny with sweat in his drenched workout clothes.

Marge would be proud of how she was gathering the data.

"Do you mind if I join you?" he was saying, even as he lowered his long frame down to the rough surface of the rock, taking the place Scout had cleverly vacated by circling around to Bridey's other side, blocking her from moving away.

"Not at all," she said, surprising herself, realizing she really didn't mind. Without the glowering manner and the ultra correct, button-down attire, he was actually a very desirable male, especially in his abbreviated clothing.

As his body came close to hers and there was the lightest brush of his leg against hers, she was startled to feel a palpable connection between them, as though an electromagnetic field had come to life between his body and hers. A good feeling it was, exciting and alive, yet full of safety and comfort. The surrounding temperature seemed to rise by about ten degrees. She felt as though she was melting.

*What's going on?*

And Mack was asking himself a similar question. *How does she do that?*

For he felt it, too, as though some magical switch had suddenly been flipped, sending a powerful message through him. He felt all his faculties focus, all brought to attention, aware and sensitive in a way he'd never before experienced. Again, he asked himself, *How does she do that?* He studied her glowing face, as though he might find an answer there. *Maybe it's her mouth. So soft, so innocent. Or maybe it's the perfect complexion.* He'd never seen a sunlit feathering of freckles look so sexy. How many girls could look that good in bright sunlight? He knew that the women of his social set avoided the sun's rays as though they expected to shrivel; their careful makeup was designed to guarantee their nighttime beauty under the subdued lighting of expensive restaurants and Broadway theater houses.

But this girl was unafraid of the light.

The backs of his knees were tingling, and he could feel something tightening in his chest, as though a fist was gripping his heart. The edges of his ears were burning, and he felt a powerful impulse to touch her face with his fingertips, to reach an arm around her, draw her slim body closer to him . . .

*What's happening to me?*

His next thought was even more direct.

*Am I going to get involved with this woman?*

*Impossible. No way.*

But he felt his usual aplomb swirling down the drain, and he had to use all his well-practiced self-discipline to mask his confused feelings, to force himself to sound casual. He made the only innocuous comment he could think of.

"I've been smelling good things coming from across the hall," he said, as casually as he could. "You can't be doing all that cooking just for yourself."

"Oh, no, of course not," she answered, glad of the turn the conversation had taken. He couldn't have picked a better topic, guaranteed to bring out the shine of dedication in her eyes, and safely removed from the startling reaction he'd triggered in her. "It's for a project I'm working on: a cookbook. I donate everything to a service that collects food for the homeless."

"Most commendable," he said. *And she can cook, too!* "So you're writing a cookbook," he said. "How long have you been working on it?"

"I just started. But one chapter is already finished. The first draft, at least. With a kitchen like the one in that apartment, I should be able to complete the whole book in a year. If I'm lucky."

He felt his heart sink. This was getting too complicated.

"A whole year? That's a long haul you've got ahead of you."

"Not really. I've got the perfect place to get it done. That apartment is a dream. And I've never seen a kitchen like that, not in a private home. You can't imagine—"

The fates really weren't playing fair. But someone would have to tell her. He steeled himself. Might as well get it over with now.

"I hate to be the bearer of bad news," he said, "but someone should have told you."

She felt the temperature drop suddenly, alarmingly.

"What do you mean?"

"I mean you're not going to be able to stay in the apartment."

"What are you talking about?" Her stomach went hollow and she gripped the solid rock beneath her, which seemed to turn to knives and spikes, pricking at her.

"Didn't the people who hired you warn you?"

"Warn me?"

Now he was glowering again.

"They're really not being fair to you," he said, "letting you get started on a big project. Letting you get your hopes up."

The hollow in her stomach spread up through her chest as she heard a threat to all her plans . . . all her work . . .

"Maybe you could explain—"

He suddenly felt rotten. Explain? Explain that, because of him, she could just toss her plans out of the window? He'd seen the color drain from her face and the sudden tension that appeared like a shadow in her eyes. Not that he'd ever been one to shy away from tough confrontations, but all of a sudden he was feeling like a really bad guy, and he didn't like the feeling at all. He needed to think this over and he couldn't think very clearly, not with this glowing girl so close to him. He tried to summon up his powers of self-command, but there was a buzzing in his head, as though all his thoughts had turned into a flight of disoriented bees. It was so damned complicated.

His fists clenched, he squinted into the sunlight, keeping his mouth clamped tight.

*I need to get out of here,* he thought.

Reflexively, defensively, he glanced at his watch. Then he glanced at her. Then back at his watch, as though its face might give him some direction. Then he did an uncharacteristic thing. He chose the path of least resistance. He chickened out.

He stood up, and the dog stood up to join him.

"I've got to be going now," he said. He brushed off his shorts. "Come on, Scout," he said.

Her mouth was open and her hand was raised, as though to stop him.

"But—"

She couldn't let him just leave her like that. Not after dropping such a bombshell on her.

But Mack climbed down the rock with Scout right behind him. As casually as he could manage, he added, over his shoulder, "I think you'd better give that lawyer a call. He has some explaining to do." He started running down the path, but when he'd gone only twenty yards, he stopped and called back to her.

"Hey, I don't know your name!"

"It's Bridget. Bridey. Bridey Berrigan."

"And I'm Mack. Mack Brewster."

He turned and started running again, but as he blended into the stream of runners, she heard him call back, "I'll be seeing you, Bridey Berrigan."

And then he was gone.

## Chapter Five

Bridey was dizzy with confusion. One minute she'd been sitting next to Mack and feeling all warm and toasty, and the next, all the good feelings had been scared right out of her. The lighthearted pleasure of the morning had drained away, and even the glowing sunshine seemed to have lost its warmth.

Work! Work was what she needed. Her project, the most important thing in her life, was now apparently at risk, and it seemed suddenly more important than ever. With a sense of doom looming over her, she jogged the few blocks back to apartment 12A, where *Breads and Rolls* was waiting for her. She showered quickly and, leaving her hair only towel-dried, pulled on a pair of panties and covered up with nothing more than a super-long T-shirt. In the kitchen her bread doughs were well risen, and in minutes she was hard at work, forming loaves, buns, cinnamon rolls. While the first batches baked, she sat down in front of her computer.

She typed out her chapter heading, centering it neatly on the screen:

And then, on the next line she typed:

Don't Panic

Shrinks cost pots of money. So do health clubs and aerobics classes.

But making bread costs practically nothing at all, and it gives you all the benefits of free therapy—plus a good workout.

You get to slam the dough around and hear the satisfying thunk as you beat it into submission, you get to assert your authority, shake the walls and, at the same time, release all those awful "aggression toxins."

And you produce results that will dazzle everyone: family, friends, even that cute guy next door—

Her fingers had typed those last words before she realized what she had written. Startled, she sat back and reread the last phrase.

"I can't believe I wrote that," she said aloud.

"Meow?"

Silk, who'd been prowling nervously around the kitchen all morning, seemed glad of a little conversation, and Bridey, full of fidgety tension, was glad of a chance to lighten up a little.

"None of your business, Miss Has To Know It All. Can't a girl keep any secrets around here?" Bridey glared at Silk. "Just because you've been as jumpy as a cat lately doesn't mean everyone else has to be in a state. I've got worries of my own, and you don't see me carrying on, do you? Honestly, if anyone should be prying, it should be me. Don't think I haven't noticed how loopy you've been acting. So what's up with you these days? And why aren't you taking your snooze, like Satin over there?"

In his dreams, Satin heard his name mentioned. He twitched one ear, half-opened his eyes and then slipped back into heroic visions featuring himself on the trail of a ferocious mouse. *It's a dirty job,* his dream self explained to his dream audience, *but someone has to do it!*

"Meooww?" Silk was not to be put off. She pawed Bridey's bare toes insistently.

"Oh, go take a catnap!" Bridey said. "And leave me alone. Sure, Mack Brewster has good legs and a sexy smile, but he's no hero. He's got me really worried, and I really have to get this work done as fast as I can, before it all gets taken away from me. So just go away and leave me alone!"

She looked back at the screen, hit the delete button and took out the last words.

And then typed them in again. She couldn't help it. They seemed to fit.

". . . the cute guy next door . . ."

She had to admit it—she couldn't get him out of her head, and it wasn't only because of his warning of trouble in her paradise. Or because of the strange magnetic field, or whatever it was, that she'd felt when his leg touched hers. There was something more about him, something deep in his eyes, something . . . something about the tone in his voice, a kind of strength that reached out to her, as though he had taken her hand; it stayed with her still.

*Do I like this guy?*

She sat back in her chair abruptly, as though her spine had collapsed.

The thought appalled her.

Still, there was something . . .

*That's all I need. A major distraction, just when I need to be totally devoted to work! No. I'm not about to give it all away. I'm not going to let myself get derailed. Don't think about him, Bridey. Don't.*

But it was like telling herself not to think about elephants. She stared at her computer screen, but she couldn't get past ". . . the cute guy next door . . ."

And just then, as though her thoughts had summoned him, the doorbell rang and, when she answered it, there he was.

He was now in crisp chinos and a neatly pressed denim shirt. His handsome face was freshly shaved, his shower-damp hair was neatly combed and he was wearing a serious, best-behavior expression.

"I was just wondering," he said. "Could it possibly be cook's night out?"

He'd caught her completely off guard and she was speechless. She was embarrassingly aware of her super-casual attire, the huge T-shirt and only panties beneath, just this side of decency. With one bare foot she tried to restrain Silk, who was determined to escape through the open door.

Before she could say anything, he added, "I mean, is it safe to ask a professional chef out to dinner?"

His eyes were wandering over her barely clad figure and, realizing her discomfort and recognizing its cause, he was kind enough to focus on a spot in the middle of her forehead. He kept his smile to himself.

Bridey bent to scoop Silk up into her arms, using her as a protective cover across her chest.

"Uh, I'm not sure," she stammered. "I mean—that is—I guess so. Uh, what did you have in mind?"

His eyes drifted down to meet hers, but he managed not to say what was really going on in his mind.

"I was thinking," he said, "we really need to talk."

"Well . . ."

"I feel maybe I should explain . . ."

"Explain?"

"Maybe we could have dinner? Perhaps, if you'd like, the Cote d'Or?" He paused hopefully. "Tonight? At eight?"

"Well, I guess. That is, sure. That would be . . . swell."

*Swell?* She'd never used such a word in her whole life. She knew she was thoroughly discomposed.

"Great!" he said. "See you then."

"Eight o'clock," she repeated. He was still standing there, practically at attention, as she closed the door.

Bridey hugged Silk close, burying her face in the sleek fur as she walked aimlessly through the huge apartment, wandering unseeing from room to room.

"Oh, Silk," she whispered into the cat's soft ear. "I don't know what to think."

Silk reached her soft face toward Bridey's own silken cheek, encouraging her to tell all.

"He really is the most—"

But her about-to-be-revealed confidence was interrupted by the ringing of the telephone. She looked around, only then realizing she was in the library. Marge was already talking as Bridey picked up the phone on Neville's desk.

"It's a gorgeous day." Marge sounded bubbly. "Perfect for shopping, and there's a super sale going on at Saks. Can I lure you away from your labors for an afternoon?"

"No way, Marge." She set Silk down onto a burgundy leather chair and watched her jump down onto the Persian carpet and scamper away. "Gotta work. Things may be falling apart here, and I have to finish as much as I can before—"

"Oh, no! Don't tell me some long-lost relative turned up to claim the inheritance."

"Nothing like that. But Mack says—"

"Mack?"

"The guy next door."

"Oho! So you know his name. We're making progress!"

"Well, yes and no. The bad news is there may be something funky about this job. Mack says it won't last long, not long enough for me to finish the book. He seems to have some kind of insider information."

"Uh-oh. That is bad." There was a moment's pause. "So what's the good news?"

"The good news is he's taking me to dinner tonight. At the Cote d'Or. That's my chance to find out what's happening."

Marge squealed. "The Cote d'Or. Oh, Bridey! That's fabulous!" Then her voice dropped an octave from girlish glee to conspiratorial seriousness. Seriously serious. Marge's mental social computer was running at warp speed. "Listen, honey. This man must be really well connected. You can't get into the Cote d'Or without a reservation months in advance. Do you have time to get your nails done?"

"No, Marge, I don't have time to get my nails done. And I'm not going to make the time, either. Bad enough I'm taking off time for dinner. Anyway, he's already seen me looking like a scullery maid. It doesn't seem to bother him." Bridey looked at her poor hand with its little burns and nicks and scrapes. An occupational hazard; nothing to be done about it.

"All right, all right. No need to panic."

"I'm not panicking, Marge."

"I know. I know, dear." Marge took a deep breath, audible to Bridey. She was regrouping. "What are you going to wear? Something slinky, I hope."

"I don't have anything slinky."

"I can lend you something."

"I don't need anything. I'll be fine. We're just going to have dinner, for goodness' sake. My basic black will do. I'll wear my Grandma's locket."

"Well, think sexy. That's the best way to accessorize."

"Oh, Marge, you're too much. I hardly know the guy."

"And he hardly knows you. That's the point. You want to let him know there's more to you than Danish pastry. God, if I had your shape . . ."

"I'll keep it in mind. And now I've got to go. I've got bread in the oven and a chapter to finish."

"Okay. But remember, think sexy!"

# Chapter Six

The cloisonné clock in the library struck eight, the oven timer went off, and the doorbell rang, all at the same moment. Bridey stopped in her tracks, in mid-kitchen, with pot holders in her hands and cake racks at the ready.

"Omigod!" she whispered to the cats. "He's here!"

Silk and Satin had been prowling around her feet for the last half hour, getting in her way as she simultaneously dressed for her date and put a low-fat coffee cake to the test. She'd been making a comical spectacle for them as, without missing a beat, she'd brushed her teeth, pulled on panty hose, finished her computer notes, and slipped into her basic black sheath.

"I should have known," she said, slipping eight hot cake pans onto the waiting racks. "He would be perfectly punctual, of course. He must have been waiting out there with a stopwatch."

She tossed the pot holders onto the counter, turned off the oven and raced to the door, stopping only long enough to grab one fast look in the foyer mirror, where she patted her hair, checked to be sure there was no lipstick on her teeth and, remembering Marge's advice to think sexy, ran her hands quickly down the black dress, making sure it lay smoothly over her body.

Then she took one deep breath, slowed herself down, and opened the door.

His suit was dark, his shirt was crisply white, and his repp tie was old school: blue and black stripes on red. His Burberry raincoat was draped over his arm and he carried his umbrella in one hand. He was the very image of gentlemanly propriety. Still, and to her enormous surprise, only one word flashed through her head.

*Sexy.*

Instantly, she felt a flush rising in her cheeks and knew it would show. With her light coloring, Bridey never had been able to hide a blush. Embarrassed, she saw his eyes do a quick scan of her from top to bottom before coming to rest on her pink cheeks, and she prepared to blame them on the hot stove she'd been slaving over all afternoon. She turned away to hide her face.

"I'll just get my coat," she said, stepping back from the door and pushing at Silk, who was trying to scoot past her.

"Mmmm," he said, sticking his head inside the door. "Smells good in here."

The aroma from the kitchen was flooding the hallway.

"Coffee cake," she said as she succeeded in getting the door closed behind her without de-tailing Silk.

"My favorite," he said as he rang for the elevator. He took her coat from her and, as he helped her on with it, he caught the scent of her hair, which smelled deliciously of cinnamon. Visions of spicy muffins danced in his head.

Which is not to say he hadn't also noticed the dress. He had noticed the dress. And the flushed cheeks. And the beautiful eyes, and the light from behind her that lit up her hair. Only one word flashed through his head.

*Sexy.*

The Cote d'Or couldn't intimidate Bridey. She knew too much about restaurants and what went on behind the fancy fronts. She knew exactly what it took to put on this elaborate show of elegance and sophistication, the enormous displays of fabulous hothouse flowers, the always spotless linens, the perfectly polished brass fixtures, the candles set at each table to cast a romantic glow on the diners' faces. She understood the costing out of every half-teaspoon of salt and every splash of balsamic vinegar. She knew the frantic activity that was hidden from the public, the mundane mechanics that made the fantasy possible. She knew the unobtrusive signals that indicated special treatment for a preferred diner and his guest, the way their coats were taken to be checked, the maître d's almost intimate attention, the serious conference with the wine steward, the careful choices of courses for their dinner.

She also knew haute cuisine when she tasted it,

and the *escalopes de veau* on her plate were as haute as they could get on their bed of couscous, raisins, and prunes, prepared in the Moroccan style, a combination of sweet and tangy that sang of the Casbah and hot desert sands.

And, while Bridey checked out the veal and couscous, Mack checked out Bridey, looking her over, comparing her to the other women he dated. What he saw was that Bridey Berrigan was totally at ease. She had none of the self-conscious preening and haughtiness that his usual dates brought with them, the preoccupation with their furs and jewels, their hair and nails. Involuntarily, he glanced at Bridey's hands and saw all the little marks of her kitchen work. For some reason, they seemed very sweet, very appealing.

The realization hit him like a fist in the chest, hard.

*This one is a real woman.*

It took his breath away. Mack Brewster wasn't used to being blindsided.

Meanwhile, Bridey had given the first forkful one professional taste of appreciation and now was ready for the real reason for this dinner.

"You dropped a bombshell on me this morning," she said, looking him straight in the eyes as she lifted a second forkful to her mouth.

*What was it she'd said? About a bombshell?*

Mack wrenched his thoughts back under control, remembering why he'd asked her to dinner. She deserved an explanation. Of course. But suddenly the explanation seemed harder than he'd expected.

"More wine?" he said, grasping at anything to cover his momentary confusion. He signaled the waiter, who was standing at quiet readiness near the wall.

"You're not avoiding the subject now, are you?" she asked while the waiter poured the silky Bordeaux into her glass. "You said yourself, we need to talk."

"I'm not avoiding the subject," he said, irritated by his own irresoluteness, irritated by how easily this little slip of a girl—this cook!—was getting under his skin, making him nervous. "I'm not avoiding the subject," he repeated, convincing himself. "Not at all. It's just that I realized when we talked this morning that you'd been set up for a bad disappointment, and I thought I ought to let you in on what's happening."

Bridey lost all interest in her dinner. She was focused now only on Mack, whose face seemed to take on an almost devilish appearance in the candlelight's glow.

"What's happening?" She felt her pulse quickening.

Mack sliced his steak and chewed down a mouthful before continuing.

"The thing is," he said at last, delivering his bombshell as casually as if he was sprinkling salt on his steak, "it's my intention to buy that apartment myself, as soon as possible. I'm going to break through the walls and take over the whole floor." He cut through another slice of meat, focusing his attention on it more than on her. "I've been planning this deal for a long time—ever since my dad died—and now that old Mrs. Willey is out of the picture, I'll be able to go ahead immediately. I'd have done it years ago if she'd agreed to sell, but she was such an obstinate, bad-tempered old bat." He waved his knife above his plate as though he was cutting right through Mrs. Willey. "Oh, she was full of charm and grace when she was being the grande dame. You saw her portrait. That was the gorgeous side of Henrietta Willey. But just let the world not spin in her favor, then you'd see the imperious diva she really was. Then the claws would come out, and if you crossed her, you'd better watch out. And she could hold a grudge forever."

Bridey's veal had turned to straw and she couldn't touch another mouthful. Panic bubbled up in her like a balloon and she struggled to fight back.

"And in those last years," he continued, "she'd gotten totally batty."

"But what on earth would you do with so much space? A single man, all alone in that enormous place, just you and your dog—"

"The market is soft right now and I can get that place at a good price. I mean to do it before someone else snaps it up. Anyway, I don't expect to be alone forever. I'll get married someday, and I expect there'll be lots of kids to fill up all those bedrooms."

"But no one can snap it up. Silk and Satin own it, and I think they like it. It's been their home for years and—"

A shadow of sarcastic superiority passed over Mack's face.

"So you talk cat?" he said dismissively, still chewing.

"The cats and I have gotten very close," she said. Now she was feeling defensive. And ridiculous.

"Yeah. Well, no matter what those cats *think,* I've got news for them. They don't quite own it yet—not while there's a will to probate. And there's no way that crazy legacy is going to stand up. The co-op board won't allow it."

"The co-op board? What have they got to do with it?"

"They're not going to tolerate letting a couple of pussycats remain as the sole owners of their prime unit." His tone was totally sarcastic.

"You mean the board's going to challenge the will?"

"I think they will. I think I can convince them to do it."

"You?"

"Sure. I'm on the board."

"And you have that much influence?"

"I think I do."

"But that isn't what Henrietta Willey wanted. Doesn't her will mean anything?"

"Not if it's completely nuts. And I mean *completely* nuts."

He looked so sure of himself, she wanted to punch him.

"And just how long will all this take?"

"Not long. A month or so, my lawyers tell me."

She was dismayed to find it had gone so far already.

"And then I'd have to leave?"

The bubbles of panic turned into a flood. *He doesn't get it,* she thought. *He doesn't get it at all.*

"I'm afraid so, Bridey. That's the only part I'm sorry about. I know it means a lot to you to finish your book."

"No, you don't know. You have no idea what it means to me."

Visions of hundred-pound potato sacks and huge, greasy tubs of boiling soup swam past her.

He saw the tears welling in her eyes, and he looked startled. He reached for her hand. She pulled it away.

"No, you don't have any idea," she repeated angrily. "None at all."

He was totally disconcerted by the sudden twist in the conversation.

"What did I say? Bridey, I wasn't trying to upset you. I just thought . . . this morning in the park—"

The waiter came and cleared their places to prepare them for dessert. He put a plate of tiny cookies on the table.

Again, Mack reached for Bridey's hand, this time closing it firmly over hers, feeling its warmth, trying to control its resistance. And again she yanked it forcefully away, determined.

"Please, Bridey. What can I do?" He hadn't anticipated such a fierce reaction, and he cast about for some way to stop this disastrous development, for some way to make it up to her. Confused, he picked up a fragile Florentine from the plate of cookies and offered it to her. "Here," he said, "have a cookie."

It was the last straw. She covered her eyes with her napkin and ran to the restroom, leaving him sitting there totally befuddled.

*What did I do?* he asked himself as he ate the cookie himself. *What did I do? What did I say?*

The restroom was a pink and white confection. There were mirrors all around, a damask-covered settee against the wall facing the marble-topped washstands and fresh flowers blooming in a crystal vase. Near the entrance, an elderly woman wearing a shiny black uniform and a tiny white apron waited attentively, a cluster of hand towels draped over one arm, ready to offer any assistance. When she saw Bridey's face, she averted her eyes discreetly and found something to do in the next room, where the stalls were. She'd had this job for six years and Bridey wasn't the first young woman she'd seen run weeping into the restroom, needing to get away from everyone.

Bridey didn't even notice the attendant. She dropped onto the settee and stared disconsolately at her image in the mirror opposite.

*Oh, that big jerk,* she thought. *He's ruining everything. My big chance. I need a year at least, probably more. Just when I thought everything was going so well. But what does he care? Just so he can have some huge space to play around in. He'd probably get rid of all that beautiful furniture, all those antiques. Paint everything battleship gray, I bet. I can just see it: he'll turn the living room into a gym. For a family he doesn't even have. Just him and his big dog!*

And what about the cats? What about those two sweet, beautiful animals? What would happen to Silk and Satin?

She imagined them tossed out into the street like a couple of strays. A tiny laugh broke through her tears.

*Silk might get a kick out of that,* she thought ruefully, remembering Silk's adventure at the fish market.

The thought of Silk slinking around in dark alleys, having the time of her life, restored Bridey's perspective. Silk wouldn't go weeping into the ladies' room just because life tossed a hurdle or two in her path.

*Get over it, Bridey,* she told herself sharply. She went to the washstand and dabbed cold water at her eyes and pulled herself together.

"Some *sexy!*" she whispered to her reflection. "He wouldn't have cared if I'd worn a brown paper bag. Mack Brewster's only interest is the apartment. He's got his own plans, and he's not concerned with anyone else's." She sniffled once. "It's a good thing I didn't waste time getting my nails done."

She realized the attendant had peeked around the corner to see if it was safe to return.

She dried her face.

"Let's just get back there," she ordered her reflection in the mirror, "and finish up this dinner. Then let's get out of here as fast as possible."

Mack rose from his seat as she returned to the table and reached for her chair to hold it as she sat down. He opened his mouth, but she spoke first.

"What about Silk and Satin?" she asked, totally composed, totally chilly.

"The cats?"

"Yes, of course, the cats."

"Oh, I don't know. I'm sure some provision could be made for them. They're nice cats; someone would want to take them. If not, they could go to the ASPCA. Or Bideawee, or some such organization."

"Nice cats? They're not just nice cats. They're wonderful cats. They're special cats. They're beautiful and sensitive cats. And 12A is their home, the only home they've ever known, the home they're entitled to remain in. That's what Henrietta Willey wanted for them, and she made very clear and specific arrangements for them. They can't just be tossed out on the street. Don't you have a heart?"

"Of course I have a heart, Bridey." He looked befuddled. "And I love all animals, great and small. But I already have Scout, and I'm not going to ask him to share his space with a couple of felines. He might object."

By now she was getting mad. And madder still, every moment. Her own stubbornness had been aroused by Mack's air of unqualified self-assurance.

"Well, it's not his space yet. And it's not your space either. And you know what? This space is getting too small for me." She glanced around the quiet room. "I would like to go home now."

"But you haven't had your dessert." He looked dismayed. "At least have some coffee."

"I don't want any coffee." She stood up. "And I don't want any dessert." She had her bag in her hand and was already headed for the door.

Mack practically knocked over his chair, digging

in his pocket for some cash and signaling the waiter to bring the check. She was out of the door by the time he'd tossed some bills onto the table. By the time he'd retrieved their coats and his umbrella from the checkroom, he had to run to catch up with her.

"Now, dammit, Bridey," he said, reaching her side as she strode down Hudson Street, looking for a cab. He was trying to assert the control he was so accustomed to. "Now, dammit, I won't allow you to go off mad."

"You won't *allow* me?"

She turned to flash an outraged glance at him.

"I didn't mean that." He said it quickly, awkwardly, like a man stumbling over his own feet. "I only meant I wanted this to be a nice dinner. I wanted us to get to know each other. I only wanted to explain about—"

A cab pulled up and he grabbed the door, holding it for her.

"Oh, just go away!" She was practically snarling.

She yanked her coat out of his hands, got into the cab and pulled the door closed behind her before he could join her. She flounced back against the seat and folded her arms indignantly across her chest.

"Six Twelve Park," she snapped at the driver.

And then she was silent.

And Mack, left alone in the middle of Hudson Street, with the cars weaving around him, threw his hands into the air and spoke to no one in particular. "What did I do? What's she so mad about?"

He really didn't get it.

Was it a guy thing?

## Chapter Seven

Bridey needed to calm down and regroup. Slamming the door behind her, slapping her bag angrily onto a chair, glowering fiercely at the hall mirror as she passed it; none of that helped. Anger had been overtaken by anxiety. She kicked off her shoes, plunked herself deep into the pillows of the pale silk sofa and pulled her feet up under her. Silk and Satin jumped up next to her, and she gathered them close for comfort.

"What will I do?" she whispered into Silk's ear. "If I lose this place, I'll have to start all over again. I'll have to find another apartment, go back to a restaurant job, postpone everything while I save my money again. Oh, Silk, everything seemed so perfect."

The telephone's ring interrupted her.

As usual, Marge didn't wait for any greeting. "Can we talk? Are you alone?"

"Of course I'm alone, Marge. What did you expect?"

"Oh, something romantic, I guess. How did your dinner with your uptight friend turn out?"

"Just awful, Marge. Worse than awful. And Mack Brewster is no friend of mine. Just wait till you hear." She told the whole dreadful story while Marge murmured little gasps of surprise, sympathy and support. "If that man manages to get me out of this apartment, I'm in real trouble. I don't know what I'll do."

"You know you're welcome to stay with me."

"You're sweet, Marge, but that doesn't solve my problem. Or the cats' problem, either. But thanks anyway."

"But it's so sad," Marge said, "the way he turned from hero to wicked villain just like that."

"He was never a hero, Marge, just a good-looking guy who happens to live next door . . . and who also happens to be planning to put me out of house and home. But now at least I understand why he glared at me that first day, like he had something against me before we'd even met. He did have something against me. I was in his way; I was trouble, a nuisance in the way of his plans." With each word Bridey was making herself madder. "I was just an inconvenient hurdle he needed to jump over. He only took me out to dinner tonight so he could tell me he was planning to get rid of me."

"Wow, that was real big of him."

"Wasn't it, though?" Bridey said sarcastically. By now she was really furious.

"Anyway, did you find out?"

"Did I find out what?"

"Did you learn anything more about him? What's his business . . . what is he, a lawyer, a politician, an interior decorator? Is he living off a big inheritance? Maybe a playboy with a trust fund? He's got to be well fixed if he's got an apartment in that building."

"I have no idea. It never came up, and I didn't think to ask. I had other things on my mind. But I'm pretty sure he's not a decorator," she said with a little laugh. "There's nothing at all artsy about him. I can't imagine him fussing over a bolt of paisley print. Anyway, I can't worry about that now, Marge. I don't care if he's a tinker, tailor, soldier or spy. For me, he's just trouble. I'm going to have to work at top speed from here on, and right now I have eight cakes to check and a day's worth of notes to write up."

"Well, keep me posted. I gotta go now, too. Gotta get my beauty sleep."

They said good-bye, but Bridey didn't head for the kitchen right away. Instead, she remained curled up in the corner of the sofa, stroking Silk's back. There was something deep inside her heart that was stabbing at her painfully, a confusion of anger and anxiety, along with a persistent memory of Mack's voice, his smile, a sense of his authority that wrapped itself protectively around her.

It made no sense. It made no sense at all.

She let her fingertips feel the reassuring, sensual

pleasure of Satin's responsive movement under her hand as the cat snuggled warmly up against her, purring softly.

Bridey imagined having to leave this wonderful apartment and suddenly realized that in the short time she'd lived here, it had become more than just a wonderful opportunity; she had come to love it for its beauty, its elegance and perfection of taste, for its gracious comfort. Without knowing it, she had allowed it to become her home. Her eyes wandered around the room, as though she needed to store up in her memory each beautiful thing here, the glow of the lamplight on the fine old woods, the silver and crystal objects that decorated the room, the silk upholsteries, the Persian carpets.

And then, and not for the first time, her gaze rested on the portrait of Henrietta Willey that hung above the fireplace. There was something about the portrait that had drawn her, irresistibly, from her first day there, as though it held some special message for her, something loving and magical. The picture had been painted long ago, when Henrietta hadn't been much older than Bridey herself was now, and in its vibrant, amused expression Bridey could see no resemblance at all to the irascible and reclusive old woman Henrietta had become. The girl in the portrait wore a gown of sea-foam green satin that billowed luxuriously about her, showing off the slim grace of her lithe figure, with a filmy lace stole draped casually off her white shoulders, her long, slim fingers clasping it loosely before her. A cloud of glowing, tawny-blonde hair surrounded her dramatic face, and her expression radiated a lively and gregarious energy and a warmth that invited intimacy. What turn in Henrietta's life could have soured her into the mean-spirited, isolated woman she'd become?

*Even so, I think I would have liked to have known her.*

The room was dark beyond the single light next to the sofa, and outside lights sparkled from thousands of windows. They reminded her that there were countless individuals out there, each with their own concerns, each of them unconnected to the other, each untouched by her problems.

She went toward the kitchen, turning on the lights in each room as she passed through.

Two hours later, after recording the results of her day's work, she was finally ready for bed. It was time to put aside her worries, at least until the morning, and she decided she badly needed some pampering. She logged off her computer and put it to bed for the night.

"A hot bath," she said to the cats, who were settling into their beds. "A long, bubbly soak in the tub, just the thing to make me forget Mack Brewster and the ASPCA. That and a glass of warm milk."

But despite a long, relaxing soak in the bubble-filled bathtub, and despite a lavish, all-over application of lotions, the man next door remained on her mind. Even as she snuggled into bed with a magazine and her glass of warm milk, she couldn't forget him. Her feelings were more complicated than she could understand. Sure, Mack was the heavy in this piece, but still . . . what was it? A feeling of loss that had nothing to do with eighteen rooms and free rent and a fabulous kitchen. What was it about him—was it only his intelligent face, his secure masculinity, his confident, self-assured bearing—she remembered the way the candlelight from the table had softened the rugged planes of his handsome face and added a depth to the texture of his black hair, the way his dark eyes looked into her own . . .

She slammed shut the door on the image.

She turned the pages of her magazine. But her eyes took in nothing of what was on them.

Finally she gave up trying to read. She finished her milk, turned out the light and burrowed her head into the pile of pillows. And in the dark, she realized that Mack Brewster was in the apartment next door, only a few feet away from her.

He, too, she thought, must be in his bed, sleeping nearby, separated from her by only a wall. She wondered what his bedroom looked like. She wondered what he wore to bed—probably an old-fashioned nightshirt, she thought, making herself laugh by adding a floppy nightcap to the image—

she wondered if he also drank warm milk before going to sleep, or if he said his prayers, or if perhaps he was thinking of her . . .

She sat up abruptly, grabbed a pillow and threw it hard at the wall opposite her.

"Damn that man!"

Then she slumped down under the covers.

"Damn that man," she whispered into the dark.

But Mack was not in his bed. For the last hour he'd been sitting in a deck chair on the terrace of his apartment. With Scout sprawled beside him, their two forms concealed by the night, he'd been watching the lights in the windows of apartment 12A. He knew when Bridey finished working in the kitchen and turned out the light, and he could see her shadow behind the drawn curtains of the bedroom windows as she moved about inside, getting ready for bed.

He wasn't spying on her.

He just couldn't get her off his mind.

## Chapter Eight

It was a cool Monday morning, and Gerald Kinski was just getting out of his topcoat when the intercom on his desk buzzed.

"It's Miss Berrigan on one, Mr. Kinski."

He hit the speaker button.

"Morning, Bridey. What's up?"

He tossed his coat onto the leather sofa, settled into his chair and picked up the receiver. While he talked, he fingered through the stack of weekend mail that was waiting for him on his desk. He frowned as he picked one envelope out of the pile and read the return address. Could this be the reason for her call?

"Would you have a couple of minutes for me to come by this morning?" Bridey was saying. "I need to talk to you."

"Is there a problem?" he asked.

"Maybe," she said. "Would ten o'clock be all right?"

He glanced at his watch. "Sure, Bridey. I'll be able to fit you in at ten."

"Thanks, Mr. Kinski. I'll be there in an hour."

He waited for the dial tone and then rang his secretary.

"Cynthia, Bridey Berrigan will be in at ten. Give us about thirty minutes. And would you ring Harold Maudsley for me?" He looked at the paper in his hand and read off the phone number to her from the letterhead. "He's on the Six Twelve Park Avenue co-op board."

"So, Bridey, what can I do for you?"

Gerry settled back into the depths of his chair and smiled at her. *She is such a treat,* he was thinking. *She brings the springtime in with her.*

Her miniskirt was pale green and dotted with tiny yellow buttercups, and her cropped yellow blouse had a row of little buttons marching down the front. She made him think of a spring flower, just opening up to summer's sunshine. She carried a darker green jacket and laid that over the arm of her chair.

"Well, Mr. Kinski, I'm not sure how to say this, but I think I have a problem."

"Yes, you said that when you called. Everything's okay with the cats, I hope."

"Oh, sure," she said nervously. For a moment she thought of confessing to him about Silk's little adventure at the fish market but decided she'd better not say anything about that. "Silk and Satin are just fine. We're getting along great. No, it's about the apartment."

Gerry nodded his head.

"I know you didn't make any promises, but I did hope to stay long enough to finish my project. But now something's come up. I'm worried that this job isn't going to last much longer. If you can tell me anything, I need to know, because it's really important to me to be able to finish my work."

*Damn,* he thought. *News sure travels fast.*

"What have you heard?" he asked.

"I met one of my neighbors," she said. "Mr. Brewster."

She meant to say no more than was absolutely necessary, so she left out the part about their meeting in the park, their aborted dinner date and his arrogant assumption of his own rectitude—and how his black hair fell in soft waves at the back of his neck, just clearing the top of his shirt collar, and how surprisingly sexy and masculine a man could look in a conservative suit and a casual raincoat . . .

All of that was racing helter-skelter through her head, but she made herself focus on her reason for being there.

"Is it true?" she asked coolly, giving no hint of her distress. "Is the co-op board going to contest the will? Can they do that?"

"Well, it would be unusual, but it looks like they might try." Gerry picked up the paper from his desk and scanned the list of board members' names printed on the letterhead. There it was: Mackenzie Haven Brewster. "How do you know Mr. Brewster?"

"Oh, Mack lives in Twelve B," she said, making it sound casual. "We just happened to meet in the hall."

"Mack?"

"Mr. Brewster, I mean." She felt the flush rising in her cheeks and cursed the fair complexion that had always been such a dead giveaway. She rushed on with her explanation. "He told me he's been planning for a long time to buy the Willey apartment—"

"All that in the hallway?"

"Well, uh . . ." She came to a stammering stop.

Gerry smiled slightly. He had seen the bright color rising in her cheeks and heard her nervous stammer.

*So,* he thought. *The plot thickens.*

He kept that thought to himself.

"This just came in the mail," he said, heading her off. He waved the letter in his hand. "The board is notifying me that they do indeed intend to challenge that portion of the will that concerns the apartment. They say that the passing of the property to anyone other than a family member is contrary to the co-op rules." He saw her face go pale again and wished the board had been a little slower about coming to their decision. Brewster must be pushing them. Maybe he'd already made an offer on the apartment. "I'm sorry, Bridey, but it looks like we may have a fight on our hands. I'd like to see you stay there as long as you want. And our firm had hoped for as little publicity as possible—"

He cut himself short. The whole matter had been embarrassing right from the beginning and he certainly wasn't prepared to reveal his own foolishness to anyone outside the firm. Increasingly, as he got older, there were days—and it looked like this was turning into one of them—when he wished he could retire to his place in the country, maybe take up some sort of soothing hobby. Wood carving might be nice . . .

"Mr. Brewster says he wants to break through and take over the whole floor."

*He told her all that,* Gerry thought, *just chatting in the hallway?*

"And what's more, he's planning to just turn the cats out. He'd send poor Silk and Satin to the ASPCA or something—"

*That must have been some conversation. She practically got the man's life story.*

"—as though Scout deserves to be in that apartment more than they do."

"Scout?"

"His dog. His black Labrador retriever."

Gerry thought this all over for a long moment. Then he asked, "What more do you know about this Mack Brewster? What's his business?"

"I don't know."

"Sounds like we ought to find out." Gerry wondered why she'd missed out on that.

"Does it matter?"

"You never know. I'll check it out and let you know if it's important." He made a few notes on a yellow pad. "In the meantime, you should just go on home, Bridey, and continue your cooking and writing. These legal proceedings take time, and if there's one thing we lawyers know how to do, it's how to slow things down. Nothing's going to happen for a little while, anyway, and we'll drag it out as much as we can. See if we can't stall things enough so you can finish your book. You just go on home and continue as you were."

He came around to her chair and handed her the green jacket as she rose.

"And everything's okay with Silk and Satin?" he asked as he walked her to the reception area.

"Oh, sure. They're just fine. No problem."

"Good. We want them to enjoy every one of their nine lives." As they shook hands at the door, he said, "How long do cats live, anyway?"

"I don't know. Fifteen, twenty years?"

The door closed behind her.

*Good. I'll be safely retired by then.*

Gerald Kinski was not alone in dreaming of an escape into retirement. A few blocks away, in the offices of Harmon & Brewster, Helen Goodman was fuming. She yanked the chair back from her desk.

"I've been that man's executive secretary for three years," she said, slapping down a folder full of papers, "and for his father for thirty years before that, and no one's ever spoken to me that way before! Maybe I'm just getting too old for this job." She pulled a tissue out of the box in her bottom drawer and blew her nose loudly. "If he doesn't want me around anymore, maybe it's time for me to take my pension and get out of here."

"Oh, Helen. Everyone knows this place couldn't run without you."

Janet Warensky had just popped into Helen's office for her regular 10 a.m. coffee break. She'd brought two mugs with her, just filled from the brewer in the kitchenette down the hall, and she set Helen's in its usual spot, next to the African violets that always bloomed on Helen's desk.

In her many years as Harmon & Brewster's marketing manager, Janet had seen all sorts of crises come and go, but she'd never known her friend to be in such a state.

"Mr. Brewster's always so even-tempered," she said. "What happened?"

Helen was too upset to even hear the question.

"I've known that boy since he was in diapers." She blew her nose again. "I remember when his mother used to bring him in here when he was just a baby. He used to play around everyone's feet, pushing his toy cars across the carpet. He was Scooter back then, not Mr. Brewster. Why, I still have the birthday cards he used to draw for me. How could he talk to me like that?"

"Like what? What did he say?"

"I'd left these letters on his desk for his signature." She pointed at the folder. "He barely looked at them and he just threw them back at me, right across his desk." She mimicked Mack's deep voice sarcastically. "'These are a mess,' he said. He practically barked at me. 'What's the matter with you, Helen?' he said. 'Can't you do anything right?'"

"Mr. Brewster said that? To you? Why, Helen, your work is so meticulous. And it's so unlike him to talk that way. He's always so polite and correct."

"And then he said, 'Just take these and get out of here! Just get the hell out of here and leave me alone!' Well," she went on indignantly, "no one talks to me that way! I've a good mind to hand in my resignation this minute."

"Oh, don't do that, Helen. I can hardly believe it of Mr. Brewster. Something must be bothering him. Maybe it's a girl. Maybe he's been seeing someone and he got dumped."

"There isn't any girl. I'd know about it if there were a girl. He'd be sending flowers and things. Remember when he thought he was in love with that Tiffany Glover? That snobby young lawyer from Baines and Dunster? Remember how he was on the phone to her every couple of hours? But he never acted like this when they broke up. Oh, sure, he moped around for a couple of days, but—"

The door behind her opened and Mack was there.

"Helen, could you come in here, please?" he said sharply.

She wiped her eyes, squared her narrow shoulders and got up.

"Of course, Mr. Brewster," she said, as coldly as she could. He held the door for her as she went into his book-lined office.

"Please sit down, Helen."

She did.

He pushed aside a tall stack of papers and sat on the corner of his desk, facing her.

"My behavior was inexcusable, Helen," he said rather stiffly. "I'm very sorry. I should never have spoken to you that way. I'm just not myself today."

"Well, Mr. Brewster . . ." She noticed that his tie was slightly off center and one button on the collar of his button-down shirt was undone. No, he certainly wasn't himself today. As though in confirmation, Mack looked down at his tasseled loafers and frowned, as if he was seeing them for the first time that morning. Casual brown shoes with a dark gray business suit. Whoever he was today, he was definitely not himself.

"Please accept my apology," he was saying. "It has nothing to do with you, Helen. Your work is always excellent."

"Thank you, Mr. Brewster. I try to do my best."

"I know you do, Helen, and Harmon and Brewster couldn't get along without you. *I* couldn't get along without you."

Maybe, she thought, she wouldn't retire just yet after all. She stood up to go.

"You can bring those letters back, Helen," he continued, "and I'll sign them. Just check the spelling of Colin Balfoure's name. I think he spells it with an *e* at the end."

"Yes, Mr. Brewster." She was feeling much better now. Mack was still glowering, but at least not at her.

"And then get me Harold Maudsley on the phone, at the co-op board. You have the number?"

"It's on my Rolodex."

As she reached the door, he added, "And Helen, after you do that, would you send a dozen roses to Miss Bridget Berrigan, at Six Twelve Park. Apartment Twelve A."

*Oh!* She felt triumphant. *So it is a girl, after all!*

"No, wait. On second thought," he said, "not roses. Roses are too formal. Tell them to make up a big arrangement of spring flowers: freesias, daffodils, that kind of thing."

*Oh, boy! Here we go again.* "Yes, Mr. Brewster. And will you want to enclose a card?"

"Oh, that's right. A card." He pinched his lower lip thoughtfully and then said, "I'll write it out for you and you can read it to them when you call in the order."

She waited while he scrawled his message on a memo pad. After a moment's thought and a couple of false starts, he handed her the note and she closed the door behind her.

She took it to her desk, where Janet was waiting expectantly.

"So," Janet said, "did he fire you? Or has the storm passed?"

Helen finished reading the note and handed it to Janet.

"You were right," she said. "Look at that."

*The guy I live with,* it said, *can sometimes jam*

*his big foot in his mouth and not even figure out how it got there. Please rescue him before he chokes to death.* It was signed *Scout.*

"Scout?"

"His dog."

The two women grinned at each other conspiratorially as Helen picked up the phone.

"Do you think this is the one?" Janet asked.

"I sure hope so. It's about time that man settled down."

# Chapter Nine

"He just caught me totally off guard, Marge."

Bridey had her cell phone in one hand and Mack's card in the other, and she was pacing around the kitchen, practically wearing a tread in the floor tiles. The huge bunch of cheery spring flowers confronted her from the countertop, where she'd set it down in the middle of her working mess. She had been creating *Stews on Sunday, Dinners All Week*, and had all six burners going when the flowers arrived.

"What should I do, Marge?"

"Oh, give the guy a chance," Marge said. "At least talk to him. Talk is a good thing."

"I don't know, Marge. After last night—"

"Look, sweetie, I'd love to hold your hand through this, but I've got layout people coming in now, and one of our editors left a manuscript at her kid's nursery school. Somewhere up in Westchester, no less. It's crazy here and we have a Wednesday deadline. I just can't talk now."

"Oh, sure. I'm sorry, Marge. I know you're busy. Call me tonight."

She hung up quickly.

"I know, I know," she said to Silk and Satin, who'd come into the kitchen, drawn there by the alluring aromas that had been floating out of the kitchen for the last hour. "I'm a big girl, and I can handle this myself."

Silk rubbed Bridey's ankle in agreement and Satin licked his paws as though he, for one, couldn't understand why she was making such a fuss. He had better things to do than worry about Mack Brewster's shenanigans.

"You guys don't get it," Bridey said to them. She stuck the card in among the flowers and scooped up Silk, holding her so they were face-to-face. "If you knew what that man is up to, you'd scratch his eyes out." Silk patted her reprovingly on the nose. "Well, maybe not that," she corrected herself, thinking of those handsome black eyes. "But you sure wouldn't feel friendly toward him. Or toward that big black dog of his either."

But she had to laugh. The note was kind of cute. Cuter than she'd have expected from such a stuffed shirt. Maybe Marge was right. Maybe she should give him a chance. And it wouldn't hurt to let him hear her side of things as well.

She went to her desk and, on a small piece of scratch paper, wrote:

*Scout: Even if he doesn't know how he got there, it's a smart man who knows when he's in trouble. Tell the guy you live with to stop by when he gets home from work.*

She left the note unsigned, folded it in half, carried it across the hall and slipped it under the door of 12B.

Then, with a surprising flutter inside her rib cage, like a ten-year-old girl who's just left a party invitation under the door of the best-looking boy in the class, she ducked back into 12A.

The cats, who had escorted her on her errand, returned with her to the kitchen, where a simmering Szekely goulash of pork, onions and sauerkraut had achieved a velvety, paprika-rich gloss, ready now for the addition of caraway seeds, sour cream and a generous cup of dark beer. She was feeling giddy; she made it two full cups. Then she made the appropriate notation of the change on her laptop.

"Scout says he has a message from you."

She had to laugh. The dog had her note in his mouth and Mack stood behind him, as though the roles had been reversed and he was the one on a leash.

"He brought me over," Mack said, "to say I'm sorry."

He looked spiffed up, like a boy on his way to church, in sharp chinos and a blue blazer and, Bridey noted with an inward giggle, a fresh shave. She remembered Marge's words: *Give the guy a chance.*

"I'm not sure what I did," he added, "but I'd sure like to straighten things out."

"I guess we should talk," she said, stepping back so they could come in. "Will Scout be okay with the cats?"

"Let's find out."

Bridey turned around to look for Silk and Satin, ready to grab them in the event of trouble, and broke into a laugh. Only their heads appeared around the far side of the foyer, one on either side, from the safety of the living room. They were peering out at the big black dog with cat-wary, nervous attention. Scout, for his part, was more forthcoming. He walked across the foyer and introduced himself, making a polite greeting, nose to nose, first with Satin, who, looking cautious but curious, stood his ground firmly, and then with Silk, who backed off a step and kept her ears flat, ready for fight or flight, whichever might be needed.

Mack spoke to the dog softly. "Scout, come."

Scout trotted back to his side obediently.

"Sit."

Scout sat.

"They're going to be all right," Mack said confidently. He told Scout to stay and then followed Bridey into the living room, where she retreated into the sofa's cushions, curling herself up and pulling her legs up under her. Scout remained where he'd been told to stay and the cats, after taking a precautionary look toward him, jumped up next to Bridey, staying close for protection.

Mack stood at the center of the room and looked around with a proprietary air, as though he were sizing it up for immediate occupancy, mentally removing the contents and replacing all the beautiful objects with his own belongings.

"It's been a long time," he said. "When I was a kid, I thought this place was as big as a football field. It seemed to me a plane could take off from here. Now," he added thoughtfully, taking in every detail of the exquisite decor, "it's not so intimidating." He walked over to the portrait of Henrietta that hung over the fireplace. "And old Mrs. Willey here doesn't look so formidable either, for that matter. In fact, judging from her portrait, she must have been really dazzling when she was young. You'd never know from this picture what a wicked old bat she turned into."

He turned to look at Bridey, whose delicate features, framed by the lacy froth of her lovely hair, were the equal of any artist's portrayal: the casual grace of her slim form against the sleek fabric of the sofa, the perfect contrast her vivid coloring made with the pale decor of her surroundings, her ease with the cats, who were resting companionably against her, made a picture as beautiful as the one above the fireplace, as though the whole room had been specially designed to show her off like a precious gem in an exquisite setting. For a moment, his imagination dressed her in finery to match Henrietta's, in a gown and jewels, and once again, as on that morning in the park, he was astonished to feel his hand tingle with the urge to trace one of the soft curls that cupped her ear, to entwine a copper tendril around his finger. He almost reached out to touch her.

*What a pity,* he thought, feeling the sudden pang of imminent loss. *We've hardly had a chance to know each other, and now . . .*

"I'm sorry if I upset you last night," he said, taking a seat in one of the low-backed wing chairs that flanked the sofa. "I just thought it was only fair to tell you that I expect to take over this apartment pretty soon so you can plan accordingly. I didn't know you were counting on being here for a long time. The lawyers should have explained that to you. But really, does it make such a difference? Surely you'll be able to finish your work somewhere else."

He said it so casually, so indifferently. She

realized he hadn't a clue. He was the picture of self-confidence, his tall, handsome body at ease in the graceful chair, his place in the world safe and assured. He'd never known the kinds of financial worries she faced, the fearful hole she'd dug for herself, burning her bridges, quitting her job, putting all her savings into her expensive electronic stuff, taking this leap into insecurity, all on the fragile hope of writing her way into a better life. Mack Brewster took wealth and comfort for granted; she, on the other hand, would have to put all her dreams on hold, go back to the back-breaking work she'd determined to leave behind her . . .

"It's not that easy," she said. "I don't think you'd understand." The anger she'd felt last night was flaring up again, but she remembered what Marge had said.

*Talk is good. Give him a chance.*

He was gazing at her, his black eyes exploring her face, waiting for her to continue, and once again her thoughts and feelings tangled up into a knot of confusion. How could it be that she felt something very comfortable about him, something that didn't square with her anger and resentment?

And Marge's words kept repeating themselves.

*Talk is good.*

Maybe she should try. Maybe he would understand.

But what difference would it make? She was

nothing to him. How could her dreams be of any importance to a man so obviously accustomed to getting his own way? Her thoughts were all tumbling around in her head and she didn't know where to start. It takes courage to bare your soul, and Bridey was hardly eager to expose her vulnerability.

And then she really surprised herself; she chickened out. But only temporarily, she insisted to herself.

"Excuse me," she said, changing the subject abruptly. "I have to stir a pot."

She got up, and Satin and Silk jumped down from the sofa to follow her.

"Can I come too?"

Mack stood up.

"If you like," she said, feeling relieved that she'd deflected the immediate problem. *Later,* she thought.

He signaled to Scout to come along, and they all trooped down the hall to the kitchen, with the cats keeping a nervous distance from the big black dog.

"It smells wonderful," he said. "It takes me back many years. I can remember when there was always something good going on in this kitchen. We used to be able to smell it from across the hall." He pointed to the big stockpots bubbling away on the stove. "What are you making?"

"Stews from around the world." She had picked

up a wooden spoon, ready to stir, and used it to indicate each one in succession. "Szekely goulash from Hungary in that one. Doro wat from Ethiopia there. Mexican chili con carne. Swedish beef with capers and beets and egg yolks. Mongolian mutton stew. And a beef bourguignon from France. Can't have good cooking without something from France."

"Aren't they awfully complicated?"

"Not at all. That's the whole point. Each one can be made easily. And if you make a big pot, you can freeze individual portions. So if you've got a family and a busy schedule, the kids can pitch in on a Sunday afternoon, all the cooking for a few weeks is done in one shot and then everyone can go cruise the mall. Saves a ton of money, lets the family do something fun together and then everyone eats like royalty. Of course, you don't all eat chili or goulash every night. You can mix them up, just pop whichever ones you want into the microwave, and have something different for each person, something different whenever you want, and you don't have to order in pizza all the time. Even for singles, who are cooking just for themselves, or if friends drop in."

She was off and running on her favorite subject, and her enthusiasm made her cheeks glow and her eyes light up even beyond their usual sparkle.

"But that's not the real point of my book. I'm trying to write for an older generation too. I hear so many mothers complaining that their grown-up kids don't know how to cook at all, that they don't turn on their ovens from one end of the year to the other, that they can't even peel a potato. I want them to see how life has changed for young people today, that a salad bar and a packaged sandwich is about all a tired girl or guy can manage after a hard day at the office. I want my book to be broad enough to reach mothers and their daughters. And their sons too. I want—"

He interrupted her. "You're making me hungry." He smiled appealingly, like a kid trying to maneuver an invitation.

And Bridey, who couldn't be mad at anyone in her kitchen, astonished herself by asking, "Have you had dinner?"

The words had popped out before she could stop them. *What am I doing?* she thought, realizing her words had implied an invitation.

"I'm so glad you asked." He grinned suddenly at her. "I'll set the table. Just point me in the right direction."

This was not at all what she had planned, but the pleasure of sharing her food overcame everything else. She concealed her confusion by bending her head over a pot and lifting the lid to check the contents, letting the savory steam surround her face like a protective shield. She stirred, dipped up a test spoonful and managed to retrieve her cool demeanor.

"Plates there," she said, putting the cover back on the pot and pointing at one of the cabinets. "Forks there. I'll get the napkins."

She sliced several pieces of bread from one of yesterday's loaves and set them in a basket on the table. She dropped handfuls of lettuce, already washed and waiting in the refrigerator's crisper, into a salad bowl, tossed in a splash of peanut oil and a spritz of Japanese rice vinegar, added a few dashes of salt and some twists of pepper and gave it all a quick toss. Then she turned on the light that hung above the table and dimmed the big working lights in the rest of the room, creating a soft glow around the little dining table. Twilight was approaching, and outside the kitchen window the birds were beginning to roost in the magnolia trees on Mack's terrace, singing their day's last song. Scout settled down near Mack's feet. Silk and Satin were drinking from their water bowls. The pots were bubbling on the stove.

*It feels like a family dinner,* Bridey thought.

The sweetness of it hit her in the middle of her chest with a thump, like the impact of a drumbeat.

Meanwhile, several floors below, another neighbor was in serious need of just such a quiet evening at home. Harold Maudsley was already on overload. What with his busy law practice, his heavy-duty social life and his various civic commitments, his days were hectic enough; the additional duties he'd taken on as president of the building's co-op board made the "honor" more of a hassle than it was worth. Against his better judgment, he'd allowed the board to prevail on him to volunteer for the position because he'd felt an obligation to make his legal expertise available, even though he didn't really have the kind of time the job demanded. What's more, his wife was getting tired of hearing him complain about all his co-op problems. He wished he hadn't let them rope him into the whole thing. He poured his pre-dinner martini and settled heavily into his favorite chair.

"And now here's Mack Brewster," he said, looking at her over his newspaper, "after all that table pounding at our last meeting, after all his insisting that there mustn't be any delay in challenging Henrietta Willey's crazy will: now here he is all of a sudden calling me to say there's really no need to rush. I don't know what's gotten into the man."

Harold had been in court all day and hadn't picked up Mack's message—along with twenty others—until he'd returned to his office at six o'clock, too late to reach Mack at work. Now, at almost eight o'clock, while they waited for the cook to get dinner ready, it was among the day's many irritations he was reviewing for his wife.

Vivien Maudsley didn't even look up from her *Vogue* magazine.

"Maybe he's changed his mind about buying the

apartment," she said absentmindedly. She stroked a languid hand along her sleek, ash-blonde hair, careful not to muss its upswept perfection. She couldn't care less if Mack Brewster moved into 12A or not. "What in the world does he want with that place anyway? It's much too big for him alone, and he's already got that perfectly good space next door."

She sipped her drink and continued her reading, turning the pages with carefully sculptured nails, causing the gold and diamonds on her fingers to flash a most satisfactory light. As far as she was concerned, letting those two stupid cats occupy the residence was outrageous.

"If you ask me," she added abstractedly as her eye was caught by a spread of the latest from Givenchy, "I think you should just go ahead and get those cats out of there so some real people can move in."

"Well, that's just what I'm doing," Harold said petulantly. "The whole thing is crazy. Leaving all that money and a whole apartment to a couple of pampered pets when living space in New York is so limited." His tone was all indignant righteousness, conveniently ignoring the fact that there was no shortage of multimillion-dollar apartments in the city. "Anyway, he was in such a stew about it at the last meeting, I went ahead and filed the papers right away. It's all been taken care of." He looked at his watch and then picked up the phone that lay on the end table. "I'll just give him a call and let him know."

But he only reached the answering machine at Mack's apartment, so he left his message and hung up. With that done, Harold Maudsley poured another martini and settled back to read his newspaper in peace. The cook would have dinner ready in about twenty minutes, and he needed the time to wind down from his exhausting day.

And in the kitchen of 12A, Mack's steely resolve had vanished he knew not where. He'd intended only to make a friendly, neighborly visit, clear up any questions Bridey might have, lay his plans on the line, smooth any ruffled feathers, and then retreat, skirmish won.

Instead, the evening's magic was working on him, and here he was, enjoying the best dinner he'd had in a long time and feeling an inexplicable need to share with this bright sprite of a girl the whole, long story, a story he'd never told anyone. Perhaps it was the golden light or the quiet of the evening. Perhaps it was the perfect chili. But he didn't know how to begin. Perhaps he should postpone—

"About the apartment . . ." Bridey's words interrupted his thoughts.

There it was; he knew he couldn't put it off.

"Right," he said. "About the apartment." He stared into his chili but found no help there. "I was just trying to figure out where to start."

"Is it so complicated?"

"Oh, yes. It's very complicated. Henrietta's crazy legacy. The apartment. The cats. And now . . ."

He came to a stop, distracted by the play of the light on her fine features, the way it shadowed her high cheekbones and gleamed softly along the delicate line of her jaw.

"And now?"

"And now, you," he said awkwardly. "I didn't expect—" He stopped himself, feeling as if he was about to say more than he meant to, and he covered it up by adding teasingly, "You should have been a dried-up old crone with a wart on your nose."

"Sorry about that," she said testily. "I've got a few years yet before I get to cronehood. And anyway, warts don't run in my family." She took a bite of bread. "But go ahead," she said. "I'm listening."

He took a deep breath. "Well, like I said, it's complicated. It goes back a long way. Ten, twelve years. Maybe more."

"I don't get it," she said. "Satin and Silk can't be more than a couple of years old."

"Oh, it has nothing to do with the cats. They were just a handy vehicle."

"A vehicle? For what? What do you mean?"

"Her way to keep me from getting the apartment."

"I don't understand." Bridey peered intently at his strong features, the determined set of his jaw, the intelligent, thoughtful depth of his dark eyes. She was touched by the way the lines of humor around his mouth softened his air of authority and command. To her surprise, she really liked what she saw: the conservative cut of his wavy black hair, the understatement of his oxford shirt, the perfection of his well-tailored blazer, all expressing the same comforting sense of solidity, of strength and security she'd felt when they'd sat together on that rock in the park.

*He doesn't exactly have pizzazz.* She imagined herself reporting the whole thing to Marge. *I don't exactly know how to describe what it is that he does have. But he definitely has something . . .*

He had put down his knife and fork and rested his elbows on either side of his plate, locking his fingers together and leaning toward her, pressing his mouth against his hands. The words were so hard to find.

But, finally, he began.

## Chapter Ten

"To begin with," he said, shifting awkwardly in his seat, "the twelfth floor isn't divided symmetrically."

"So?"

*Why is he starting way out in left field?*

"So, apartment Twelve A is very large." He

waved his hand as though to demonstrate. "Eighteen rooms, including guest rooms, library, servants' quarters."

"You seem to know it well."

"I've seen the floor plan."

"You've never been in the apartment?"

"Only twice, but never past the living room. The first time was when I was just a kid. But then, after what happened—" He paused. This wasn't going to be easy.

"What happened?"

"Well, *something* happened, but I never actually knew what it was. When we first moved into the building, Mrs. Willey was perfectly cordial and neighborly. She even asked my mother to bring me in to meet her husband. She gave me a lollipop. I remember being impressed by her flamboyant manner; Henrietta Willey sure had a very dramatic way about her. She made a big show of everything she did, even if it was just giving a lollipop to a kid. And, as I said, she was quite friendly. She even asked my parents to several of her parties.

"But then, all of a sudden, with absolutely no explanation, she turned into an iceberg. Suddenly there were no more invitations. No more hellos in the elevator. No more anything. I think my mother tried to approach her about it, but when Henrietta Willey froze someone out, they stayed frozen. She was a terrifically headstrong woman and she would never have lowered herself to anything so ordinary as justifying her behavior. We just didn't exist for her anymore.

"My folks were plenty mad about getting snubbed like that, but there wasn't anything they could do about it. Of course, I was just a kid, so all of this went on kind of over my head. But eventually it became just a fact of life: the Brewsters didn't talk to the Willeys and the Willeys didn't talk to the Brewsters, and that was that."

"But what does this have to do with the twelfth floor's lack of symmetry?"

"Yeah, I guess I kind of wandered there." He paused for a moment, collecting his thoughts. "Anyway, the way it's laid out, my apartment, Twelve B, is much smaller. I have a huge terrace instead, but the apartment itself has only six rooms: kitchen, living room, dining room, two bedrooms and a maid's room. Plus three baths. That's all."

"So?" *Most people would think that's a lot.* Bridey held her tongue.

"Well, my dad had always said that someday, when I was married and had a family of my own, he wanted us all to live close to each other, with the grandkids right next door. He had these dreams—I don't know, plans, maybe—of being able to take his grandchildren to the park, buying them ice creams at the zoo, reading to them at night. He saw us all as a big extended family, with children all over the place and himself as the patriarch, seeing to it that everything was under his control, done just right."

A harsh shadow passed over Mack's face, and there was a hint of old struggles in the lines of determination that deepened around his mouth. He seemed to be looking into hard, old memories, and when he spoke again, something fierce rode beneath the surface of his words.

"And when my dad wanted something, he made sure he got it."

Bridey couldn't tell if he was speaking in pride or anger. She remained silent, realizing this was a story with many levels.

"So when Neville Willey died," he continued, "Dad decided it was a good time to approach Henrietta about buying the apartment so he could take over the whole floor. He figured this place was so big she'd be rattling around in it all by herself. He didn't see any reason why, even if she had removed us from her guest list, she wouldn't be willing to consider a good offer. It was a simple business proposition as far as he was concerned. The way he saw it, he'd be doing her a favor."

"I gather she wasn't interested?"

"Wasn't interested?" Mack laughed briefly. "She practically threw him out. She carried on some-thing awful. Mother and I could hear her yelling all the way over in our apartment. She was screaming, 'How dare you!' at my father. And 'I've never been so insulted. Of all people, *of all people!* You're the last one I'd allow to own this apartment! The very last! I'd see you dead before I'd sell to you! How dare you!' When my dad came back, he was furious. No one spoke to Llewellyn Brewster that way."

Mack's face was grim, and he pressed his clasped fists against his lips to restrain the anger the memory evoked. When he finally spoke, his eyes were hard.

"Bridey," he said intently, "my father was a tough son of a bitch. No one knew that better than I did. But he was also a gentleman of the old school, and he was accustomed to ladies who spoke softly. He wasn't about to tolerate such outrageous behavior, and he swore he'd never speak to 'that woman' again. And from that day on, he never did."

"You never found out why she was in such a rage?"

"No, I never did. None of us did."

Mack paused and looked down, frowning at his chili as though it had appeared out of nowhere. Then he sat up very straight, squaring his shoulders.

"In the Brewster family," he went on, "you stick up for your own. The battle lines were drawn, and from then on we stayed on our own side and left Henrietta alone on hers. I was about eighteen then, and heading off to Annapolis, and I guess I got caught up in my own affairs: finishing school, doing my naval service. I forgot about the whole thing. I had other things on my mind.

"But then," he continued, "a few years later, my mother died suddenly."

"Oh, I'm sorry." Bridey knew what it meant to lose a parent, and she was instantly sympathetic.

"It was while I was still in the Navy. I got word she'd had a stroke, and by the time I got home from the carrier I was stationed on, she was gone."

"That's awful."

He nodded, and his eyes seemed to lose their gleam momentarily, like he was looking somewhere into the past. "It came suddenly, with no warning at all. She'd been shopping on Fifth Avenue and was just coming out onto the street when it happened."

"And your dad?"

"Poor guy. Her death hit him awfully hard. For all his toughness, I think he needed her more than anyone realized. His personality changed completely. All that drive and power drained out of him, like he was some poor animal that mates for life and is suddenly alone, and he never recovered from the loss. He died less than a year later."

Bridey shook her head sympathetically, and they were both silent for a moment, each caught up in their own memories.

"I can sort of understand," she said, "if you feel you need to buy the apartment for his sake, but—"

"There's more to it than that," he said, interrupting her. "After the funeral, when I stood there at his grave, all I could think of was how he'd never see his dream come true. He'd never get to see his family gathered around him, his grandchildren running all around him; he'd never even get to know who they were, how they turned out. It just broke me up. It was like I couldn't think of anything else. He'd planned so carefully for his retirement years, and now he would never get to have them. I couldn't stand to see him lose out like that. I couldn't get it out of my head.

"But the final straw came when I got home from the burial. I don't know how it happened, but someone must have brought flowers to the apartment instead of sending them to the funeral home, and I guess they'd been left outside Henrietta's door by mistake. The thing is, they were all smashed, with broken-off leaves lying around on the carpet, like they'd been thrown forcibly against our door."

He paused, and his face turned to granite, as though the scene was still vivid before him.

"And there was a note," he continued grimly. "It was stuck on top of the flowers, and it was written on Henrietta Willey's notepaper, with her name engraved on it. Do you know what it said?"

He peered intently into her eyes, as though challenging her to read his mind.

She shook her head.

"It said, *Please keep your damn flowers on your own side of the hall.* It was signed *H. W.*

"It made me wild. To think she could carry a grudge so far. She must have known my father had been lowered into his grave that very morning, and she couldn't even respect that. It made me wild," he repeated. "All I could think was, 'I'll get even, you old witch!' But I knew I was too angry to think sensibly right then, so I waited a few weeks, till I calmed down, and when I did, it came to me that if I could persuade her to sell the apartment, I'd be carrying out my father's wishes. It seemed to me that in that way, at least, he could have his way this one final time. I felt like I owed it to his memory.

"So when I figured I was ready to keep a lid on my temper, I came over here to talk to Henrietta. I thought I was being very reasonable and tried to talk calmly with her. But there was no talking to that woman. She was like ice. She said she'd never forgive my father for his impossible behavior, and as far as she was concerned, she'd be glad if every Brewster in the whole world could suffer as she had, and that I would never see the day that her apartment would belong to me. She kept saying, in that imperious way of hers, 'I'll see to it! I'll see to it that you never get this place!' I guess she'd gotten totally dotty in her old age." He paused and took a long, slow breath. "So there it is. The whole sad story."

"But what could your father have done to make her so angry?"

"I have absolutely no idea. I guess it will have to remain a mystery. I don't know why I felt I had to tell you; I've never spoken of this to anyone before. Somehow, it just seemed important that you know." He laughed. "Did you put a spell on me? Did you put something in the chili?"

"No, I didn't put anything in the chili."

She laughed with him, touched by the way he had opened up to her. But now her own future was tangled up in a web of stubborn old feuds and irrational passions. Why should all this ancient history ruin her own plans?

"I'll tell you what," he said, breaking in on her thoughts. "Why don't we have dessert over on my terrace? You've never seen my place, and the view is wonderful at night."

The invitation seemed to surprise her, but not as much as it surprised him. What was it about this girl? He'd revealed himself to her as though she were his best friend in the whole world. And now, having done that, when he should get away from her before he got even more entangled, he found he was looking for excuses to stretch out the time with her.

"I don't know," she was saying. "I still have work to do . . ." *I should be avoiding you like the plague, you and your mission to take everything away from me,* Bridey thought.

But the cordial mood of the evening was still upon her, and he looked so handsome in the warm light, with his dark hair and his deep, dark eyes, and his secrets, newly revealed.

"Just half an hour," he said. "I'll make the coffee while you check out the view. It's really wonderful at night, and I like showing it off."

"Well," she heard herself saying, to her enormous surprise, "just half an hour. And I'll bring the cake." *What am I doing?*

Silk and Satin complained about being left behind, but Bridey was adamant.

"You guys stay here," she said, slipping awkwardly through the door, pushing at them with her toes. She was juggling a Sacher torte in one hand and a bowl of whipped cream in the other, while Mack held the door for her. "Take a nap or something." She barely got through as Mack closed the door against their protests. "All I need," she said to Mack, as she followed him to his apartment, "is for those two to get lost or something."

*Whoops!* She gulped and felt the telltale flush spread up her cheeks. *I shouldn't have said that!*

Mack glanced at her over his shoulder and their eyes met. The shadow of a smile caught at the corner of his mouth, and a frisson of guilt flashed through her. But if they shared a secret, he wasn't letting on and, as he held the door for her, she entered his apartment with her chin stuck up in a brave effort to express her defiance.

Mack's place was a striking contrast to the spectacular opulence of 12A. The Brewster residence was the picture of solid, lived-in domesticity. Deep chairs and a big sofa, all covered in sturdy fabrics, wore their age with assured dignity. A fine Persian rug covered part of the dark parquet floor, and leather-topped tables sat securely at strategic places around the room. Bookcases covered two whole walls, from floor to ceiling, filled with books that showed the signs of having been really read. Countless framed photos were displayed on the walls and tabletops and, here and there, mixed in with the family pictures, Bridey caught glimpses of well-known faces from the worlds of politics, science, and the arts.

One picture in particular needed no identification, although the face wasn't famous. A Bachrach portrait in a large silver frame, next to the sofa, was obviously Llewellyn Brewster, Mack's father. The similarity, despite the difference in their ages, was unmistakable: the same dark, handsome features, the same set of the jaw, the same air of authority. It occurred to her that if the son took after the father, Mack Brewster would probably age well.

Bearing the chocolate cake and the bowl of whipped cream, she followed him into the kitchen, which, though small by Willey standards, was entirely serviceable. It showed little evidence of any culinary activity, but Mack set the coffee-maker going with a few expert motions while Bridey cut the cake and dolloped the whipped cream over their portions.

"Why don't you go out to the terrace," Mack said, gesturing toward the French doors that were visible at the far end of the living room. "I'll bring this stuff out as soon as the coffee's ready."

Alone on the terrace, she surveyed the scene appreciatively. As Mack had said, it was truly huge, and no suburban patio could have been more comfortably furnished, with big lounge chairs set strategically for conversation and skyline viewing. At the center of the terra-cotta-tiled terrace was a large, round, wrought-iron table and a set of matching wrought-iron chairs. Huge planters were filled with shrubbery, along with pots of flowering plants. A whole bank of magnolia trees in full bloom filled the air with a heady scent.

She was drawn instantly to the rail-topped wall that ran around the terrace and she went to it to drink in the fabulous view. Resting her arms comfortably on the rail, she marveled at the panorama of city lights that was spread in all its dazzling glory around her. Only then did she realize that the iron railing also separated off the small portion of the terrace that belonged to the Willey apartment. With a shock, she realized that several of the Willey windows, including those of her bedroom, were visible from the Brewster side.

*Omigod.*

From here, anyone could see right into those windows.

"Looks pretty from up here, doesn't it?"

She hadn't heard Mack come out onto the terrace.

Startled, she let her attention be drawn away from those confounded windows, and she was captured again by the mesmerizing beauty of the city lights. Mack came around next to her, turned his back to the view, and rested his elbows against the terrace railing. For long minutes, mesmerized himself, his gaze rested on her face as she enjoyed the panoramic view. With her head turned away from him, she seemed to be unaware of him.

To the south, the sky-rising corporate towers marched like giant glass-and-steel robots down the length of Park Avenue. Along one side of the flower-decorated median, a stream of red taillights flowed endlessly, and on the other side, another stream of headlights flowed back toward them. Traffic lights winked red, then green, and in the distance, over the East River, a plane made its approach to LaGuardia, its wing lights flashing as it moved through the soft night.

"Yes, the city is lovely from here," she said quietly, breaking the long silence.

Mack said nothing, for he himself was entranced.

It seemed to him all the loveliness of the city was right there on his terrace. Her lively features were at rest now, but there was an animation, a kind of natural vitality that seemed to flow just below the surface, as though casting a glow from inside. The soft breeze moved gently through her hair, playfully lifting the little curls back from her face, and the terrace lights outlined the edge of her soft cheek, the arch of her slim throat, the warm curve of her delicate mouth.

Bridey was, of course, totally aware of his attention. How could she not be? Its force was palpable, radiating from him with an almost physical reality. His eyes were on her, only on her, and again, like that day in the park when his leg had touched hers, she responded to the intense, masculine presence of his body close to hers. The air seemed to grow heavier with the scent of flowers, and the traffic sounds below seemed to drift away, disappearing into the magic of the velvety night. And suddenly, she knew—oh yes, she knew—he was going to touch her; how could she not know? It was in the air, a blanket of excitement that had wrapped itself around them, an invisible bond that circled them in warm currents, connecting them inexorably.

His hand touched her face gently, as though the fingertips had a life of their own, and she turned her head toward him, leaning into that warm, strong hand. Their eyes held each other. She could feel her heart beating; she could feel her lips part slightly, as though she might speak. But there were no words. There was only the sudden thumping in her chest, only the gasp as her breath caught in her throat. And then there was only his mouth, as he bent toward her, moving closer, and then his lips touching hers, so softly, so softly . . .

Meanwhile, Satin was trying to take a catnap, in peace and quiet, and feeling put-upon by Silk's antics. What's gotten into her lately? Ever since this new person's moved in, Silk has been acting peculiar. Not that she hadn't always been a little flighty, but her behavior—which he used to find somewhat amusing—has turned downright neurotic. Take this matter of her adventure at the fish market, for example. What well-bred Russian Blue would go larking off to such low-class haunts, consorting with who knows whom, coming home smelling of perch and pike and with her fur all mussed? Scandalous! What would the old lady have said?

*Wonder whatever happened to the old lady?*

And what would she have said if she could see Silk right now, the way she was prowling around, burrowing into cushions and the corners of dark closets? Giddy one moment and irritable the next, picking fights, teasing him when he wanted to be left alone and refusing to play when he was in the mood.

Satin roused himself from his corner of the sofa, stretched languorously, arched himself up high on his four legs, yawned and then curled up again, with his face toward the back of the sofa, refusing to be bothered by Silk's incomprehensible irritableness.

You'd think, with all this new-found energy, she'd be looking thinner than she does. But just look at her: she's actually getting fat. Dreadful the way some females let themselves go.

And outside, on the terrace, Bridey was lost in Mack's arms, lost in the warmth and wonder of his kiss, in the night and the gentle breeze, knowing only the magic of his lips and the electric, pounding current that was surging through her body, making her tremble, making her forget everything, making her want to stay there forever.

She opened her eyes, and the night and the stars began to spin, slowly at first and then faster. The heady scent of magnolia blossoms wrapped her in a hypnotic veil. She felt the earth slide away.

Their lips parted, the blood in her veins seemed to boil up from her toes . . . and then everything went black.

Her knees buckled and she slumped into a dead faint against Mack's body.

His arms, already around her, tightened reflexively to hold her upright.

"Hey, there," he said. "Bridey! Jeepers!"

He was totally dumbfounded. No girl had ever fainted at his kiss.

He bent and caught his arm beneath her knees and lifted her off her feet. In a state of astonishment, he looked around for some place to set her down.

He headed for his bedroom.

Bridey's head was already clearing as he left the terrace. Scout was circling around them with his tail wagging and a puzzled expression on his face.

"What are you doing? Put me down! Mack, for God's sake, put me down!"

"You fainted."

He stood over his bed, about to set her down on it.

"That's ridiculous! I didn't faint. I couldn't have. It was the magnolias." She was struggling to get out of his arms. "Put me down this minute!"

She had turned into an awkward and unmanageable bundle, and he set her on her feet. As she stalked from the room, he followed her apologetically.

"Wait, Bridey." He caught up with her at the bedroom door and reached for her arm. "Please, Bridey. Please wait." He tried to stop her.

"What were you doing, carrying me to your bed?"

He turned beet red.

"It's not like that. Please don't think . . . I mean, no one ever fainted before . . . I mean, when I kissed them. I mean, dammit, Bridey, I had to put you down *somewhere!*" His tongue was in a tangle and she was beginning to find his confusion funny.

"And you just happened to pick your bed."

"Well . . ." He realized she was teasing him and began to smile, a nice smile that lit his black eyes with a humorous appreciation of this silly situation. "It's just that it's never happened to me before. I never had a girl pass out on me like that."

"Well, maybe it's a sign. Like I'm getting a message that I better go home now." She headed for his door. "Before I go into a coma or something."

"No! Please don't leave. You haven't had your coffee. I haven't had your cake. Please."

"Well . . ."

He rushed to take advantage of her hesitation. "I'll just pour the coffee. It'll be good for you. Just what you need to clear your head." He was already in the kitchen.

"Well . . ." She followed him halfway, winding up in the living room. "But I'm not going back on that terrace," she called to him. "Your magnolia trees are deadly." *Sure,* she added to herself. *It was the magnolia trees. Oh yeah!* She took a couple of deep breaths to steady herself.

She sat on the sofa and looked around, taking in the masses of books, the pictures, the evidence of a solid, respectable family. On the table next to her there was a telephone and an answering machine. Its light was flashing.

"You've got a message on your machine," she called to him. She could hear him moving around in the kitchen, cups rattling, spoons being laid out.

"Would you mind hitting the button?" he called back. "I can hear it from here."

"Sure." She pressed "play."

"Mack?" said a man's voice. "It's Hal Maudsley here. About eight o'clock, Monday night. Sorry I missed you. Didn't get your message till late. Just wanted to let you know, I filed those papers already. Don't worry. We'll have those cats out of there in a couple of weeks, and then the board can deal with your offer."

The message was like a slam against her heart. She looked up and saw Mack standing in the doorway, the tray of coffee cups and cream and sugar in his hands. His mouth was open and his face was the picture of dismay.

"Uh—"

Bridey stood up. "Never mind the coffee," she said sharply. The message had hit her like a sledgehammer, knocking the whole evening out of her head, bringing her own predicament back to center stage.

Mack was looking down at the tray in his hands as though he couldn't figure out how it got there.

"But—"

"No buts." She was already in the hallway and paused with her hand on the doorknob of 12B. "I've got to finish up my stews for the night. You can keep the cake. This has certainly been an interesting evening. Something to think about."

And she slammed the door behind her, hard. The pictures bounced on the walls, and Mack was left there, staring stupidly after her.

Silk came to inquire about her visit to Mack's apartment and Bridey picked her up, glad to have someone to talk to.

"'Come see my terrace,' he said. 'Look at the lovely view. I'll make you a cup of coffee.' Hah! I should have realized. He practically seduced me—with a bunch of magnolia trees yet—and it made me forget he means to take all this away from us. How could he? Oh, Silk, it's not fair!"

She pressed her forehead against the soft space between Silk's ears.

"Would you believe—oh, my dear—would you believe," she whispered into the velvet of Silk's fur, "I let that man kiss me. In spite of everything, I let him kiss me!" But she couldn't help remembering. "And when he did, it was like I went riding off somewhere out in space. Like my head filled up with air and there was music somewhere and perfume all around . . ."

She rubbed her cheek against Silk's face. She was swept up in the memory of that kiss, and her anger and anxiety got twisted into the memory.

"Oh, Silk. It was truly, really truly awesome!"

# Chapter Eleven

"You what?"

"You heard me."

"Oh, Bridey. Omigod, Bridey!"

Marge was so astonished she could only keep repeating the words. "Omigod, Bridey!" She had meant to make this a quick call between finishing her Tuesday morning meetings and diving into all the work that was waiting on her desk, but Bridey's account of last night's experience drove everything else out of her mind. The idea of fainting at a man's kiss . . . well! It was just too delicious!

"I can't believe it." She laughed. "I never heard of such a thing. Bridey, you are absolutely such a Victorian! No girl gets the vapors nowadays. It's just too wonderful. This man must be absolutely dynamite!"

"He's not dynamite. Not even! He's just a guy who doesn't happen to have my welfare at heart and who just happened to kiss me. You know, I have been kissed before, Marge. It's not like I'm twelve years old or something. It's nothing. It doesn't mean a thing."

"Yeah. Sure."

"No, really. It must have been something I ate, or something. Maybe it was the scent of the flowers." She had to laugh, too. The whole thing seemed pretty silly now. "Anyway, I think I scared the starch right out of him. He got all confused and tried to carry me into his bedroom."

"His bedroom!"

"Well, he had to put me down somewhere, didn't he?"

"Doesn't sound confused to me!"

"Well, whatever. Anyway, I came to and made him let me go. And I was out of there soon enough, before things got out of hand."

"Oh, shoot." Marge's voice revealed serious disappointment. "That is, you did the right thing, I guess. But still, it would have been sort of interesting if you—"

"Don't even go there!" Bridey interrupted her. "I don't even want to think about it. This man is nothing but trouble for me, Marge. The last thing I need is to get all weak-kneed about him."

"Bridey, sweetie, this is me, Marge, you're talking to. You can protest all you want, but I think you're falling for this Mack Brewster. Girls don't faint over just any guy, and I hear something in your voice that tells me—"

"You're wrong, Marge." Bridey brushed off her friend's suggestion. "You're just hearing your own overheated romantic fantasies. There isn't anything at all in my voice—"

She was interrupted by the call-waiting signal. "Hold on a minute," she said. "I've got another call."

She put Marge on hold, and when she clicked on the second call, she heard Gerald Kinski on the line.

"Bridey?" The lawyer sounded harried, more rushed than usual. "Bridey, I haven't much time, but I've just received some information I thought I should pass on to you. I'm afraid it's bad news."

"Bad news?" Her heart dropped.

"We've just received notice that the Six Twelve co-op board is going full steam ahead with their action against the will. The papers have been served and the board is apparently serious about taking over that apartment as soon as possible. We'll fight it, of course, but I have to say I think their case isn't entirely without merit. They've sent me a copy of the bylaws and the Willey proprietary lease. It's all a lot of legal mumbo jumbo, of course, and I don't have time to explain it now, but here's the bottom line: they'll try to convince the court that, according to the rules, the apartment may be conveyed only to a family member. Our position will be that this is actually a transfer to a trust, which I believe is permitted by the co-op rules. Maybe, with luck, and if the judge likes cats . . ."

Bridey could hear the uncertain tone in his voice and knew he was less than optimistic about his chances of convincing anyone. After all, $70 million to a couple of pets might just raise some hackles, especially judicial hackles.

This was awful news. Gerry's phone call was dumping her even deeper into despair, bringing a hard reality still closer.

"If you can't convince the court," she said, "and the board wins, how much time will I have?"

"Hard to say. If they really push it, maybe not more than a couple of weeks."

The wave of disappointment that crashed over her was powerful enough to make her gasp. She felt tears welling up and had to force herself to remember that she was no longer a little girl; she was old enough to know that disappointments are part of life. But oh, it really was hard. Everything had started out so beautifully, and now this!

"I'm really sorry, Bridey."

"I know, Mr. Kinski." Silk and Satin had come to sit next to her, as though they knew she needed comforting, and as she stroked their backs, they arched against her in sympathy. She forced back the tears and kept her voice as normal as she could. "I know, and I appreciate your calling to let me know. Do you think I should start looking for another place?"

"Oh no. I don't think so, not yet. Let me feel them out and see if we can at least get a delay before we have to go to court. If they don't have a firm offer from a buyer lined up yet, they may be willing to slow things down a little. Give you a little extra time."

Her eyes went to the wall, as though she could see through to the apartment next door.

"I wouldn't count on them not having a buyer. Mack Brewster wants this place, and I think he's the one who's pushing them. But who knows," she added as brightly as she could, trying to muster some optimism, "maybe you'll be successful and Henrietta's will is going to stand up." If only saying it could make it so.

"That's the spirit, Bridey. Please be assured we'll do our best."

"I know you will, Mr. Kinski."

"Oh, by the way . . ." He'd been about to hang up and then remembered something else. "Speaking of Mack Brewster. I had my associate do a little research and here's what we found out about Mackenzie Brewster's business. His father was Llewellyn Brewster, one of the founders of Harmon and Brewster Publishers. They're one of the oldest publishing houses in New York. When Llewellyn died, his son took over the firm."

*Publishing. So that's what he does. I should have guessed, from all those books in his place.*

"The firm's been around for ages," Gerald continued. "They handle scholarly works mostly, nonfiction and research materials. History, political science, that sort of thing. Very solid company, and very, very posh. The son seems to be in the family tradition, deals only with the most intellectual stuff. I hear he's supposed to be very staid and conservative. My sources tell me he went to all the right schools, did a tour in the Navy, belongs to a couple of good clubs. Gets seen around town with some of the usual bright young women, but no one steady. *New York* magazine covered him last year in an article on New York's new crop of eligible bachelors. Thought you might like to know."

"Thanks, Mr. Kinski. I'm sure he's a very upright individual." She tried to keep the sarcasm down, but it was an effort.

"So that's all for now. I'll keep you posted, Bridey. In the meantime, you keep working away. Maybe everything will turn out just fine."

She tried to sound upbeat. "I hope so."

They both hung up.

Bridey stared out of the window, feeling resentful that outside the day was full of sunshine. Shouldn't it be dreary and gray, with at least a little rain to mirror the gloom in her heart? Just when everything seemed the most bleak, just when she felt the most embarrassed and frustrated by the events of the previous evening, betrayed by her own emotions, threatened by the apartment-greedy co-op board and its legal maneuverings, why was New York wearing its cheeriest attire, its trees turning bright green under a crystal sky, the happy jingle of an ice cream truck reaching up to her from far below, singing of summer's approach? Why, when her career and all her dreams were threatened, was the city putting on its most optimistic face? Even the potted geraniums on the balcony outside the French doors seemed especially vivid.

The phone rang again.

*Omigod! I forgot Marge!*

But it wasn't Marge. It was Gerald Kinski again.

"Sorry to bother you, Bridey, but just after I hung up, a registered letter was handed to me. More bad news, I'm afraid. Are you sitting down?"

Her heart sank still further. It seemed to be stuck somewhere around her navel.

"Is it that bad?" she asked. A sparrow flew onto the balcony railing and began to chirp away merrily, and Satin went to investigate. Silk jumped down from the sofa, too, and joined her brother in the sunshine. "Is it so bad that I have to sit down?"

"It may be."

Involuntarily, she stood up and started pacing in circles.

"Okay. I'm ready."

"The letter is really amazing. It's from attorneys representing someone named Afton G. Morley. Claims to be a relative of Henrietta Willey from somewhere out west, in Idaho."

"But I thought she didn't have any relatives."

"Must be someone she didn't know about. Says here 'first cousin twice removed.'"

"But how did this Afton Morley know about the will?"

"I have no idea. But they've apparently got

documents to authenticate the relationship. If this is legitimate, we've got new problems."

"Afton. What kind of a name is that? Male or female?"

"The letter doesn't indicate."

"So what does this Afton, he or she, have to say?"

"The letter says he—or she—is coming to New York to examine the apartment, see what the property looks like. Asks for an appointment on Friday here in my office, and then a trip uptown to see the place. If you don't want to be there, Bridey, you can be out for a few hours. What do you think?"

"No, that's all right. I'd like to be here." Like the crazy compulsion to drive into oncoming headlights, she was drawn irresistibly to seeing Afton Morley in person.

"Okay, if you're sure about that. I'll call you first so you'll know when to expect us."

She clicked off the phone and stared desolately into space.

"Oh, great," she said to no one at all, "it seems like everyone is ganging up on me. First the co-op board, then Mack and now this new person. Everyone seems to be trying to get me out of here." She couldn't hold back the tears now, and they fell in big drops. Silk came and rubbed her sweet face against Bridey's ankles, and she pulled her up into her lap.

"And if any one of them succeeds," she sniffled

mournfully, "you and Satin will be out of here, too. You don't understand that, do you?"

She dug her fingers into Silk's blue-gray fur and gently scratched the deep pelt at the back of the cat's neck.

"You're just fat and sassy and totally without a worry in the world, aren't you? Oh, sweetie, if you only knew what's happening here."

The phone interrupted her again. She wiped her wet face, brushing away the tears, and forced her voice to sound steady.

This time it was Mack. "Listen, we really do need to talk," he said. His voice was a mixture of contrition, eagerness, and command. "About last night—"

"Never mind last night," she said. Despite her misery, a sudden, triumphant thrill raced through her. It had just occurred to her: Now she had something that would rattle his chains, instead of the other way around. "I've just had some news that concerns you," she said.

"Oh?"

He must have caught the one-up tone in her voice, for she could hear him come up short, like a cartoon character suddenly digging his skidding heels into the dirt. The comical image made her feel better instantly.

"Yes," she said. "It's about your campaign to capture this apartment. It's just run into a major road block."

There was a short silence while he took that in.

"What are you talking about?" he said finally, his tone cautious.

"Gerald Kinski called me not more than a minute ago. You'll never guess what it is."

"Don't play games with me, Bridey." Now he sounded impatient. "Just tell me what he said."

Oh, how she wished she could draw it out, tease him a little, let him stew in his own impatience for a minute. But her news was bursting out of her and she couldn't contain it.

"A relative has turned up."

"A relative?"

"Yes. A relative of Henrietta Willey, with a claim against the estate. Someone out west, apparently someone Mrs. Willey didn't know about. He—or she—is coming here on Friday to see the apartment. So I guess this changes things considerably."

There was silence on the other end, so she went on. "Of course, this changes things for me, too," she said.

There was still no sound from Mack.

"If their claim is good, I'll be out on my ear, and I don't know what I'll do."

Silence.

"Mack? Are you still there?"

"I'm thinking."

"What are you thinking?"

"I'm thinking the co-op board has an interest in all this," he said thoughtfully. "Someone should be there on Friday to represent the board. I'll talk to Harold Maudsley first, but I think he'll want me to be on hand when this person arrives."

"Why not? The more the merrier. It'll be a regular party," she said sarcastically.

"Then it's a date. I'll see you on Friday."

"Sure. It's a date."

## Chapter Twelve

Friday's first light came up pale blue and white across the East River, striking the tops of the skyscrapers of Midtown Manhattan into flashes of brilliance. But ominous clouds were moving in from the ocean, and by midmorning the sky was overcast, turning the sun into a misted-over orb that struggled to show its face through the gray cover.

Bridey's mood was a perfect match. The prospect of Afton Morley, due to arrive at noon, was trouble enough, a regular serpent in her paradise. But the presence of Mack Brewster at the same time . . . how much stress could a girl take? She tried to tell herself that it was no big deal whether Mack was there or not, but the thump-thump in her chest was a clear contradiction. She tried all morning to concentrate on her work, but she was too wound up to get anything done and finally totally gave up all hope of finishing the chapter she'd been working on. She packed up all her notes, saved everything on her computer and forced herself to focus only on Afton Morley. In an effort to ease her edginess, she dressed casually, in a pair of black jeans and a lightweight, white cotton sweater, with her copper-gold hair pulled back from her forehead by a black headband. Then, ever the automatic hostess, she had a pot of coffee brewing by the time Mack arrived to meet their common "enemy."

They hadn't seen each other since their disastrous evening together on Monday, each managing to lock themselves behind mutually excluding walls. Mack barely nodded at Bridey as he came through the door. Bridey, for her part, was silent as she closed the door behind him.

He planted himself firmly in the living room, ready for a battle if necessary. His expression was grim. Bridey paced the big living room, feeling as though the apartment was under an escalating attack, with Mack on one flank and this long-lost relative, Morley, on the other. And it was up to her to protect it. The cats, sensing the tension in the air, had retreated to their private quarters. It was just before noon when Max, the doorman, rang up on the intercom to let Bridey know that Mr. Kinski and Mr. and Mrs. Morley had arrived.

"They're here," she said to Mack. "Two Morleys: Mr. and Mrs."

Mack's expression turned even darker. "Okay," he said tersely. "Bring them on."

He was standing at the fireplace, beneath the portrait of Henrietta. He'd left his office and come home just for this meeting, and in his dark suit and dark tie, he looked almost menacingly self-possessed.

But behind his fierce expression, a disconcerting force was percolating through him, distracting him from his single-minded determination to accomplish his mission, to honor his father's memory and acquire this apartment for his own use. It was Bridey's dilemma that kept poking at his unconscious. Though he hadn't yet realized it, her predicament had aroused his protective instincts. And when the bell rang, and he saw how bravely she squared her shoulders before she opened the door, a sympathetic pang ran through his body.

He still felt the memory of her body in his arms. And he would never forget that kiss.

"Bridey, this is Mr. Afton Morley," Gerry was saying, introducing the tall, hefty man who followed him into the apartment. "And this is Muriel Morley," he added, presenting the woman who trailed in behind her husband. "They just got in from Twin Falls last night and this is their first visit to the Big Apple."

"How do you do?" Bridey held out her hand, but Mr. Morley swept by her, striding into the apartment as though he already owned it and refusing in advance to be intimidated by its opulence. Bridey turned to Mrs. Morley, whose broad face looked a little more affable. "I hope your trip was pleasant, Mrs. Morley."

"Oh, just call me Mulie," the woman said, giving Bridey a fluttery handshake. "Everyone does. It's short for Muriel, but Afton gave me that nickname, and I guess it just stuck."

Mulie Morley was a small woman and round as a muffin. Beneath her tightly curled, ashy gray hair, her raisin-sized eyes peered out timidly from a plump, red face. The city had already scared her silly and now, entering the Willey apartment, she was awed by the magnificence that confronted her. She clutched at her straw bag as though she expected someone to try to grab it away from her and tugged at the flowery pink-and-green blouse that struggled to cover her bulky hips. Her lime-green pants strained at the elastic waistband that stretched around her ample stomach and her feet hurt from the new shoes she'd bought just for this trip. She longed to sit down and was thankful when Bridey led her toward a chair in the living room.

"Now, Mulie," her husband said sharply, "don't you go getting comfortable. We came here to see the place and we're going to get right to it."

Afton Morley was already making a tour of the room, touching things with his work-hardened fingers, lifting pieces of porcelain to examine their markings, opening drawers and poking around in their contents, as though he was taking inventory.

He'd acknowledged Mack's presence with a quick handshake and a gruff recognition of the board's interest and then paused for a moment in front of the fireplace.

"That's her, isn't it?" he said with a gesture of his chin toward Henrietta's portrait. He squinted aggressively up at it. The picture seemed to return his challenge, flashing its green eyes as though at an intruder, ready to take him on. "Must have been painted a long time ago," Afton continued, looking contemptuous. "Appears like she was a handful; full of beans, I'd say, with that red hair of hers." At this, Bridey lifted her own copper-topped head and held her chin a little higher, as though to join her own protest to Henrietta's. "Personally," Afton went on, oblivious to Bridey, "I'm not fond of difficult women. Isn't that right, Mulie?"

Mulie tucked down her chins into her plump neck. "Just what you say, Afton." Her smile, if that's what it was, was tiny.

He removed his buff-colored Stetson just long enough to smooth his thinning reddish hair and then planted it firmly back on his head, as though daring anyone to take it from him. With his pointy cowboy boots, his bolo tie and his pale blue polyester suit, he was an alien, bullish presence in this very urban place.

"So!" He planted his feet wide and stuck his hands into his pockets, pulling his jacket taut across his paunchy front. "Where are those cats?"

he demanded abruptly. "I want to see what kind of animals that damn-fool woman tried to leave all her money to."

Bridey, Mack and Gerry all exchanged glances of dismay.

"I'll get them," Bridey said. "They seem to be a little nervous today."

She left the room hurriedly, glad to escape Afton Morley's poisonous attitude.

"Nervous, huh? Never heard anything so dumb in my life, pampering a couple of animals that way."

She returned with Silk and Satin who, as soon as she put them down on the carpet, took one hostile look at the Morleys and retreated through the French windows to the safety of the balcony.

"They look pretty useless to me," Afton said, looking after them briefly. "Back on the ranch, a cat doesn't work, into a burlap bag it goes with a couple of rocks, and down to the crick."

Bridey was appalled. "What kind of work do your cats do, Mr. Morley?"

"Oh, we don't have any cats," he said dismissively. "Can't abide the fool things. But if we did, they'd catch mice is what they'd do."

He was taking a Japanese woodblock print from the wall, examining the provenance taped on its back. "Hmm," he said. "Eighteen fifty-nine. This stuff worth anything?"

"We don't have any mice here," Bridey said,

ignoring his question. She felt as though she had to defend Silk and Satin.

"Actually," Mack joined in, "Silk and Satin do have a job here. You see how they're sitting there, out on the balcony? Their job is to scare away the pigeons. Terrible mess, those pigeons make."

Just as he spoke those words, as though to make fun of them, a fat gray pigeon flew onto the railing. It hopped down to the pot of geraniums and was strutting about, clucking pompously at the cats. But the cats' attention was on the action inside the room and they took no notice of the bird at all. Afton glanced casually over his shoulder toward the balcony as he placed the print back on its hook.

"Yeah, I see how they do that," Afton said with a contemptuous snort. "I can see how those pigeons are just scared silly." Now he was holding a Limoges dish above his head, seeing how the light was diffused through the fine porcelain into a soft glow. The cats were the least of his concern. "Listen," he said offhandedly, "when I take over here, I'll just get rid of them. Can't abide the damn things."

Gerry saw Bridey's fists clench. And he also saw how Mack Brewster moved away from the fireplace to stand behind her, as though to give her moral support. There was a flash in Mack's eyes that made Gerry step in quickly to deflect this line of talk.

"Why don't we move right along?" he said. "You

wanted to see the apartment, so I'll take you through it now."

"It's about time," Afton said. "I want to see just what we're getting here." He turned to his wife. "Come along, Mulie."

"This here's some damn spread." Afton reluctantly allowed himself to be impressed. "That old girl really knew how to live it up." He'd walked through the rooms appraisingly, lifting a cushion here and opening a curtain there, feeling the fabrics roughly and even sitting down to bounce a couple of times on Bridey's bed. "Betcha it'll bring in a pretty penny when I sell it off." He waved a dismissive hand. "Can't think what anyone wants with all this frippery. Taxes alone must be a fortune. Might want to keep the place, though, at least for a few years. I may be just an old country boy, but I been doing some checking around, and I hear the market's improving here in New York. I could fill the place up with some cheap stuff and rent it out furnished till prices peak." He looked cannily around him, calculating what he could make if he sold the contents of the apartment.

"Well, Mr. Morley," Mack said gruffly, "the board has some rules about rentals of these units—"

"Why don't I show you the kitchen?" Gerry said, heading off a potential argument. "I'm sure Mrs. Morley would like to see it."

"Oh, you betcha. Mulie here's a great little cook. Tell 'em, Mulie."

"Well, they do say my ambrosia salad is something special," Mrs. Morley said timidly. She'd been silent until now and seemed uncertain about adding her two cents. "I like to add those little mini chocolate chips," she said, turning to Bridey as though revealing a girlish secret. "Gives it a little extra sweetness." She blinked her eyes several times. "Do you like to cook, dear?"

"Uh, yes, I do." Bridey didn't know what to offer against Mrs. Morley's ambrosia salad. "Actually, I do like to cook."

They arrived in the kitchen, and Mrs. Morley's mouth opened in astonishment.

"Oh, my!" she said. "I can't believe this. Not in someone's home. Why, Afton, just look at this kitchen. Oh, my! Oh, my!" She walked around the work island in the center of the room, staring wide-eyed at the enormity of it all. "Whatever in the world would anyone want with something like this, just for themselves?" she said. "I mean, Mrs. Willey never did have any children, did she? I mean, it's not like she had to feed a big family every day."

"No," Gerry said. "She never had any children. As far as she knew, she had no relatives at all." He didn't feel comfortable with this line of conversation and he tried to deflect it. "Do you have children, Mrs. Morley? You and Mr. Morley?"

"No," she said, pressing her lips together as though she anticipated criticism. "No, Afton and me, we've never been blessed with any kids. But I really love children. I come from a big family myself, three brothers and four sisters, though Afton here's an only child. I'm always telling him, he doesn't know how precious a big family is. If I could've, I'd have had a whole mob of little ones."

"Just as well," Mr. Morley said. He was looking disdainfully at all the chrome and tile and the fancy utensils. He was calculating their resale value in cold dollars and cents. "Kids are just a damn nuisance, if you ask me, unless you can get a good day's work out of 'em. And most kids today, they aren't worth what it costs to feed 'em. Anymore, it's hard to find a kid got as much as even one full day's work in him."

There was a moment of awkward silence. No one knew what to say.

Finally, it was Mr. Morley himself who filled in the gap. "But like she says, Mulie here's real big on family. Good thing she is, too, because that's how come she got into that genealogy stuff, kind of like a hobby with her. That's how we came to find out about me being Henrietta's cousin."

"First cousin twice removed," Mulie corrected him.

"Yeah. Whatever. See, one of the local papers had this piece in it about a lady in New York left all this money to her cats, and Mulie recognized the name. Lloyd was my grandpa's name, my mom's dad, so when Mulie saw that story about how Henrietta Lloyd Willey's great-great-grandpa, or some such, made all his money fur trapping out west, way back in the pioneer days, well, it set her to thinking. So Mulie here did a little research, and she tracked down how I was related to this nutty old lady. I never held much with all that genealogy stuff, seems to me a waste of time, but it sure paid off this time."

"You saw it in the paper?" Gerry interrupted him, looking uncomfortable.

"Sure did. Right there in the Twin Falls *Times-News*. Didn't you see it?"

"No, it never made the New York papers. I guess no one thought it was interesting enough." Gerry made a mental note to have one of his associates track down the item and see how it got picked up. And here he'd been thinking the story had escaped the press.

"Well, it sure got some laughs out in Twin Falls. But I got the last laugh, I guess. Me and Mulie's just gonna be laughing all the way to the bank." Once more, he removed his hat and smoothed his hair. "Anyway," he said, replacing the hat carefully, "I gotta go now and meet with my lawyers. We got us some work to do, getting all the papers signed and everything. They tell me there's gotta be some sort of hearing first. A kinship hearing, they called it. Guess they'll be in touch with you pretty soon." He paused to look into the cats' special room. "Imagine that," he said in disgust, "a whole room just for those two." He pointed at Silk, who by now had come in from the balcony and was circling her bed protectively. "What were you planning to do, put in an extra bed for each of that one's babies?"

"What do you mean, babies?" Gerry said.

"Her litter," Afton said. "That there one's carrying a litter. Can't you tell?"

All eyes came to rest on Silk. For the first time, they noticed the swelling in Silk's underbelly, the soft fur poking out all fluffy beneath her. The significance of Afton's words sank in slowly, as they realized he was right.

"Omigod!" said Bridey. "She's pregnant! How did that happen?"

"City folks!" Afton shook his head as he headed for the door. "Don't know a damn thing. Plain as the nose on your face."

Without another word, he was out into the hall, with Mulie trailing behind him, and Gerry, too, after giving Silk a long, thoughtful look, leaving Bridey and Mack alone, staring foolishly at Silk, who had settled comfortably into her bed, licking her paws and rubbing them over her nose.

*Omigod,* Bridey repeated silently to herself. *How did that happen?*

But she already knew.

*The night with Charlie Wu, buying fish.*

Mack was grinning at her. It didn't take a rocket scientist to put it all together. Did she think he'd forgotten that early morning he'd caught her coming into the building, trying so awkwardly to conceal whatever it was that was bouncing around in her tote bag?

"Looks like you'll have to 'fess up, Bridey," he said.

His amusement only made her embarrassment more painful.

"You could at least stop laughing at me," she said sharply. She was genuinely angry. "It's not funny. And anyway, I think you've got some problems of your own. Now you're going to have to deal with that dreadful man, and he may be in no mood to sell. How will you like having him and Mulie for neighbors? Maybe you'll find that funny."

Mack's face clouded over. She was right. There was nothing funny about the whole situation.

"I'd rather eat dirt," he said.

"Well," Bridey said, "you may get to try out Mulie's ambrosia salad. With chocolate chips."

He shuddered.

"So what are you going to do?"

"Well, right now the thing I must do is get back to my office. I've got a desk full of work waiting for me, enough to keep me up late tonight." He headed for the door. Then he paused and looked back at her. *I shouldn't have teased her. This must be awful for her.*

"Maybe we could try dinner again?" he suggested. "We got interrupted the last time, and we still have things to talk about."

"No!" She hadn't forgotten their last dinner.

"Are you sure? Tomorrow night? At my place? I make a mean hamburger."

"No way! I've got too much to think about."

"Maybe I can help."

She hesitated. In a way, they were on the same side now.

"Well . . ."

"Good! Seven o'clock. I'll see you then."

And he was gone, leaving Bridey with her mouth open, her thoughts spinning and the beginning of a bad headache adding to her woes.

# Chapter Thirteen

As soon as she was alone, Bridey plopped down right there on the floor next to Silk's bed and scooped her up onto her lap.

"Oh, Silk, you really went and did it, didn't you?"

Gently, she probed the soft fur under Silk's belly and confirmed what her eyes had already told her. There was no doubt; there was a plumpness there that could mean only one thing.

"Didn't anyone ever tell you to just say no?"

Bridey's headache was getting worse. She knew

she was in trouble with Gerry Kinski. And she was humiliated that Mack Brewster, of all people, had been there when Afton Morley, that smug, pompous know-it-all, showed them all up as blind fools by—oh dear, Bridey groaned in advance at her own bad pun—letting the cat out of the bag.

She let Silk jump down from her lap and sat back on her heels, watching disconsolately as she circled around the room as though she was hunting for something.

"And now I am definitely in the soup. You silly thing, don't you understand? It's bad enough I'm losing this apartment; now because of you, I'm going to lose it in disgrace."

She couldn't bring herself to add, aloud, what else was in her thoughts: that her embarrassment was that much greater because she'd been shown up in front of Mack. She felt like a bubbling pot of anxiety, as events moved inexorably against her. And floating over it all, like the Cheshire cat's smile, was Mack's smirk of knowing superiority. What did he have to feel superior about? He was about to be dumped, too. And why had she agreed to have dinner with him? What could she have been thinking?

Silk came back to her and pawed at her knees, but Bridey was too miserable to pay any more attention to her. She had calculated how long it would take Gerald Kinski to return to his office and, sure enough, right on the dot, the phone rang.

"I think we ought to have a little talk, Bridey." He sounded very serious.

"I know, Mr. Kinski. I know. I've been expecting you to call."

"So . . . do you have something to tell me?" His tone was cool and her heart dropped another couple of notches toward her stomach.

"Maybe first I should take Silk to a veterinarian," she said hopefully, "and have her examined. To make sure Mr. Morley is right."

She didn't want to face up to the question she knew was really on Gerry's mind. It wasn't a matter of whether Silk was pregnant; it was a question of how she got that way.

"Oh, I'm pretty sure he's right. As soon as he pointed it out, I could see it. But take her to a vet, by all means. Be sure to get it confirmed."

The usual friendliness was gone from his voice, but Bridey understood. He was bound to be pretty cool to the idea that she'd let Silk get out unsupervised.

"Maybe Satin is the daddy." She offered this up hopefully.

"Not possible. As soon as I got back to the office I checked his papers. He'd been fixed before Mrs. Willey agreed to take the cats. She didn't want a lot of little kittens running around the place. No, Bridey. Somehow Silk got out of that apartment, and it must have happened while you were there. So why don't you just tell me about it?"

She wished she could die.

"This isn't easy, Mr. Kinski. I'm really embarrassed."

He remained silent, and there was nothing for her to do but continue.

"She must have slipped into my tote bag one night without my knowing it. I went to the fish market and she came along for the ride, I guess." She told him the whole dumb story. "I would never have deliberately let her out of the apartment, and I didn't tell you because I got her home safely and I didn't think any harm had been done. And because I was so embarrassed. I had no idea she'd gotten herself pregnant. If I'd known, honestly, I would have told you. I swear it; I'd have told you. Honestly! I know how valuable she is, of course, and that you trusted me, and I didn't want you to think you'd hired an irresponsible jerk to take care of Mrs. Willey's cats." She could hear herself racing along, trying to explain and apologize and be reassuring all at the same time. "I'm not irresponsible, Mr. Kinski. Really, I'm not. And this job is so important to me . . ."

"Okay, Bridey. Okay."

Mr. Kinski's voice relented a bit; he couldn't help being fond of Bridey, whose appealing nature was a bright spot in his busy life, and he was touched by her obvious remorse. A bit of his customary cordiality returned. What's more, he was thinking he was hardly in a position to point accusing fingers; he knew he'd been severely remiss himself in allowing the entire situation to have come about in the first place.

"It's okay, Bridey," he said again. "I guess it could have happened to anyone. I'll have to explain it to my partners, but there's no legal harm done, I think. But take good care of those pussycats from here on. After listening to Afton Morley, I wouldn't put it past him to try to do them in. What a creep!"

"I didn't dare say it myself," she said a little timidly, "but I hate to think of someone like that taking over this beautiful place. Mack Brewster would have been bad enough, but Afton Morley is a thousand times worse. He has absolutely no appreciation of what he's getting. And he is getting it, isn't he?"

If Mack was the frying pan, she was thinking, Afton was surely the fire, and between them both, her own concerns were turning into a sizzling crisp.

"You never know," Gerry was saying. "The documents seem to be in order, but . . . well, you never know. You just never know. I'm going to go over every word in his papers with a fine-tooth comb. Something might turn up. In the meantime, you just hang in there, Bridey, and whatever you do, keep an eye on those cats. After all, we're going to have a little family soon."

Bridey hung up and took a long, slow breath.

So she wasn't in trouble with Mr. Kinski after

all. Thank God! At least one fire had been put out.

Her racing heart was slowing down to normal speed and she could feel the blood returning to her face. She turned to Silk, who was again circling the room, looking for something.

"Do you think you might manage to behave yourself from now on?"

Silk ignored her. She was busy with her own concerns.

"Now I understand why you've been so peculiar lately. And why you keep prowling around like that. Little mother! You're looking for a place to make a nest for your babies."

Silk continued prowling.

Satin came into the room, watched Silk's nervous peregrinations for a moment and then walked out again. *Women,* he seemed to be saying. Bridey thought he'd be glad when this was over and she was back to normal.

Bridey knew only one remedy for trouble; she forced herself back to work, and the rest of the afternoon passed quietly. The cats went about their own affairs, the skies stayed gray and leaden and the whole city seemed to recede into a distant, thoughtful self-preoccupation. The traffic noises that floated up from the streets below were muffled by the heavy air, and by dinner time Bridey's work on her fast-food chapter, *Salad Bars and Other Lifesavers*, was completed.

She stowed her notes, closed the computer down and prepared to make the cats' dinner. Satin stayed close to her while she got their evening meal ready, rubbing hungrily against her ankles, but Silk was nowhere in sight.

"Where's Silk?" she asked him as she set the bowls on the floor. "Doesn't she want her dinner?"

Satin couldn't care less. He was interested only in scarfing down the ground liver that filled his bowl.

"Silk?" she called. "Silk, your dinner's ready. Where are you, sweetie?" But no little Silk came running into the room. "Am I going to have to go hunting for you?" she called.

There was no response.

Bridey poured some milk into a bowl and set that down, too.

"Come on, little mother. Milk's good for you. You've got your babies to think of now."

Still no sign of Silk.

"Well, if that's how you feel, don't come crying to me when your teeth fall out and your bones melt."

Bridey felt confident that nature would take its course and Silk would show up for her dinner soon enough. She carried a bowl of veggies, a raisin-ginger scone and a Diet Coke into the family room, set a Netflix movie into the DVD player and settled down, determined to spend a couple of relaxing couch-potato hours with Audrey Hepburn and an entranced Humphrey Bogart to settle her disturbed spirits. In a little while, Satin came in to join her, curling up by her side to sleep while she watched her movie.

Maybe the film was too trivial to hold her interest. Or perhaps she had too much to think about. Her mind kept being drawn to the apartment across the hall, and she found herself wondering if Mack was at home. Or still at his office? Was his Burberry hanging in the closet, too warm for this spring day? Did he have a plan for dealing with Henrietta's long-lost relative?

Afton Morley's boorish presence still hung heavily over the apartment, as though his uncaring touch and unappreciative eye had set everything awry. Bridey found herself seeing his ham-handed intrusiveness through Henrietta's disapproving gaze, and a wave of protectiveness swept through her.

She knew Mack would do whatever he could to keep the Morleys from becoming his neighbors. But what good would that do her? In any case, she'd be the loser.

The dreadful prospect of either of them—Mack or Afton—dismantling the careful design and order of these rooms, selling off all the carefully acquired pieces of silver and crystal, the works of art, the fine fabrics that filled these rooms, was unbearable. More than ever, Bridey was identifying with Henrietta's wishes, wanting to keep this lovely place intact, wanting to preserve it in accordance with the woman's plan.

By now, she'd totally forgotten the video.

What would Henrietta have done if she could have anticipated the appearance of Afton Morley and his pumpkin of a wife? Surely she would have written her will in a way that would have blocked him from succeeding to the property, just as she had tried to block Mack.

Bridey could imagine Henrietta's fury. She could picture those green eyes flashing, the outraged toss of that elegant head, the imperious voice issuing her commands to her lawyers. If Henrietta Willey had been willing and able to intimidate so worldly and forceful a man as Llewellyn Brewster, what would she have done to Afton Morley? She'd have chopped him up for cat food!

And speaking of cat food, had Silk come out of her hiding place and eaten her dinner?

A twinge of guilt shot through Bridey's curled-up, comfortable body. After her confession to Gerald Kinski of her failure to protect Silk from her own waywardness, she felt an invisible finger poking at her conscience. She ought to be especially watchful to be sure the adventurous cat wasn't getting into any more trouble. She'd better go check on her.

She picked up the remote and turned off the movie. Satin shifted his sleek form as she got out of her chair and rearranged himself into its deep cushion. He hadn't found the movie terribly amusing and had settled himself into a pleasant postprandial nap. He was just as glad that Bridey had removed the distraction.

Bridey went into the cats' dining room. Silk's bowls of liver, milk and water were untouched.

"Silk?" she called. "Where are you?"

There was no answer. No newly plump form came running into the room.

"What are you up to now?" she said to the empty air. A chill of apprehension caught at her, running a thin, cold trail up her back. "Are you getting me into more trouble?"

She went into the living room, looked around, saw no sign of Silk. She went to the window and looked out onto the balcony to see if the cat had taken up her outpost there, from which she so often observed the passing scene, indulging her own exotic fantasies. But there was no Silk there either.

She went into the library, she went into Neville's bedroom, she checked her own bedroom, where Silk sometimes curled up against the mass of pillows that rested against the rosewood headboard. But there wasn't any evidence that the cat had been there, not so much as a warm dent in the down-filled comforter. She walked through the dressing room, pushing hangers aside and peering in among the shoes, opening drawers and poking around in them, as though she might find Silk snuggled in among her panties and bras. Still no Silk.

"Oh, come on now. This is getting spooky, Silk. Stop playing games. I know you're here some-where."

She reviewed the day. Silk had definitely been there earlier, when everyone had left. And the door to the apartment hadn't been open since then.

"You've got to be around." But still it was quiet, as quiet as it had been all afternoon.

Bridey went into Henrietta's sitting room and turned on the light. More than any other room in the apartment, this must surely have been Mrs. Willey's favorite. It was here that she wrote her letters, at a small leather-topped, Georgian writing table whose shallow drawers were filled with her engraved notepaper and formal letterhead. A brass desk lamp cast a warm glow over the chintz-covered chairs and the low, book-filled cases. It was here, with Silk and Satin at her feet, that Henrietta must have entertained her closest friends, back in the days when she still had close friends, and it was here that she must have enjoyed the knitting and sewing she did, unbeknownst to the rest of the world, which relaxed and amused her. In front of a small upholstered armchair—a Victorian piece covered in a William Morris print—a footstool rested, its fabric needlepointed, and at the chair's side was a large covered basket filled with knitting yarn, patterns, scraps and remnants of fabric. The basket's cover lay slightly askew, tipped over, perhaps, when the maid was cleaning, and Bridey bent to replace it.

Her eye was caught by the tiniest of movements inside the basket, as though a piece of velvet had shifted its position, perhaps stirred by Bridey's move to put the cover back in place. As though, but not quite. She was sure she hadn't moved the basket, and the fabric couldn't have moved by itself. Bridey stared at it and it shifted again, ever so slightly.

She pushed the piece of fabric to one side. And sure enough, a soft face looked up at her, the points of two gray-blue ears poking up from the layers of cloth. Silk shook her head and sneezed.

"So there you are! Making a nest when you should be eating your dinner." She lifted Silk up. "Let's get you out of there."

But Silk didn't want to come. Her claws dug into the surrounding remnants and dragged a few out with her, hanging like irregular little flags beneath her.

"Come on now, Silk! Don't make a mess of Mrs. Willey's basket. Let it go. You're going to rip it." Gently, she untangled the cloth from Silk's unwilling claws, holding the squirming cat aloft and ignoring her protests as bits of fabric were scattered about. "I know you think this would make a wonderful place to have your babies, but I don't think Mrs. Willey meant this basket to be a maternity ward. Come on now!"

She finally got Silk detached from the trailing pieces of cloth and sat back to survey the upheaval that had been wrought. Everything was in a multi-colored pile, a soft mass of prints and tweeds and linens. Knitting needles had tumbled out in the confusion, and scraps of taffeta and lengths of yarn were draped over the basket's edge.

"Honestly! Look what a mess you made." Bridey knelt beside the basket and picked up a piece of blue-and-white crewel, shaking it accusingly at Silk. "Now I'm going to have to sort all this out and fold it up again."

She lifted the remaining layers of cloth out of the basket and started rearranging them.

But something lay at the bottom of the basket.

A notebook, cloth covered, with a gold pen attached to it by a silk cord.

She opened it.

And read the words on the first page.

March 17, 1999
Dear Diary—

Bridey lifted her eyes from the page abruptly and shut the book.

She looked around the room quickly, as though afraid someone had seen her.

Henrietta Willey's own words! Written in her own hand! Here was a chance to look into the heart of this remarkable, self-centered and eccentric woman whose extraordinary life had drawn Bridey's into its own purposes.

But Bridey knew there is one thing you never do: you never read someone else's diary.

Never!

But—not even if the writer is no longer alive? Well . . .

She was torn. It couldn't hurt, could it? No one would ever know. Maybe just the tiniest peek, just the first page—

She half-expected lightning to strike right through the ceiling. But she opened the book again.

> Dear Diary—The book is done! I can't believe it, after all these years, I finally finished it. Nanna would have been so proud.

Henrietta's handwriting, though it suggested the copperplate style of another time—gracefully elegant and firm, the mark of good breeding and careful schooling—nevertheless sprawled flamboyantly across the page. She wrote with a broad, felt-tipped pen, and dashes and exclamation marks were strewn liberally throughout, an expression of Henrietta's characteristic self-centeredness.

Bridey felt like a clod, intruding on another's private journal, but once started, she couldn't stop herself. She went on reading.

And Mama, too. She always said something should be done to preserve all these treasures, and now I've done it. I've actually done it! Mama didn't think she was clever enough—poor Mama—she never did value herself sufficiently. She always said it would have to be up to me. Because I am [heavily underlined] clever enough! And now I've done it—I've actually written a whole book! But I could never have been so bold if it hadn't been for my darling Neville. His encouragement, his faith in me, his willingness to give me the time, without complaining— oh, my dear Neville, what would I do without you?

Bridey closed the book again, embarrassed to have stumbled so crassly into Henrietta's privacy. But the diary's lure was too great. She couldn't resist. She opened the diary again.

And now it's time, of course—time to get my book out there for all the world to enjoy! And who could know more about the subject than Yours Truly! Oh, my dear, dear diary—it feels so nervy. But,—as my darling Neville says—I've never been shy, heaven knows! But writing a book feels so revealing, such an opening of one's heart to public display. And what if the public finds that what's there is nothing more than the mediocre meanderings of a very ordinary and uninteresting person.

But <u>no</u>! [Again, heavily underlined] Banish that thought this instant, Henrietta! I, who have lived all over the world? I, who have been fortunate to be exposed to every significant event of my time, every important person of this century? Ordinary? Uninteresting? Never!

Oh, and I do so want to see my words in print. Actually in print!

Well, that's the next step. Wish me luck!

Bridey couldn't stop herself. She had to learn more. But she never expected what was revealed on the next page, across the top of which was scrawled the title:

<u>The Henrietta Lloyd Caswell Willey</u>
<u>Book of Good Eating</u>

followed by Henrietta's approving comment,

There! Doesn't that look utterly lovely?

Bridey gasped.
Henrietta had written a book about food.
There were tingles up and down her spine and

her very hair seemed to crackle with electricity, as though the writer's presence had wafted into the room, emphasizing the startling coincidence.

She needed a moment to adjust to the diary's remarkable revelation, to catch her breath, to debate with herself: should she go on reading? Was she somehow *meant* to go on reading? Did Henrietta want her to go on reading?

If ever she'd felt a bond with the departed Mrs. Willey . . .

Of course she couldn't stop herself. Who could?

Bridey took a deep breath. Silk curled up next to her, for she quite approved of the whole thing. As Bridey opened the book again, Silk peered into her face, urging her on. With one soft paw, she patted the page, placing a stamp of approval there.

"Okay," Bridey said aloud. "Here goes. And if I get into trouble, it's your fault, Silk. If you hadn't hidden in that basket . . ."

She rearranged herself comfortably on the carpet with her back against the chair and settled down
to read, the tangle of fabric around her quite forgotten.

# Chapter Fourteen

Sunday evening, March 21, 1999

Dear Diary—

Didn't sleep a wink all last night—I was so excited. Thought long and hard and finally, I've decided! I'm going to ask Llewellyn Brewster to publish my book. Isn't it lucky, my dear? One of New York's most distinguished publishers—oh, the gods must be smiling on me—to have put the Brewsters right here on my very same floor! They seem to be a nice enough couple, well-bred and good company. Mrs. B is rather quiet but very pleasant, and her husband is charming—though dreadfully opinionated—but then, I never do mind a forceful man, so much more interesting, and at least he's a gentleman. And their boy has been no trouble at all. Most teenagers set my teeth on edge, but young Mackenzie is quite acceptable. Well behaved—not like so many children these days who have no manners at all—doesn't anyone teach their children anything anymore? But this one has been well brought up—a credit to his family. Nice looking, too—he'll be quite a catch some day!

Now, my dear diary, how shall I plan my little campaign? The Harmons are coming to dinner on the 2nd—that should be a good opportunity—Jack is just back from the Middle East and will have all the news, and Edith has the good sense to let him do all the talking for both of them—and I'll ask Mimsy and Buff Nichols—their house in the Hamptons is being remodeled so they'll be in town, Buff is always good company, and if Mimsy just doesn't get off on her darling twins, God!—that woman can be such a bore when she starts gushing on and on about her babies' latest "phase"—does she really think it's so remarkable that they actually sit up in their cribs and crawl across the floor all by themselves? I'm sure there are absolutely thousands and thousands of babies sitting up and crawling all over the world right at this very minute. I'm sure, my dear, if I'd ever had any children I would never have made such an everlasting fuss over them. Such a bore! But I suppose Mimsy waited so long to have them, now she thinks they are some sort of marvels, straight from heaven. I'll just have to steer all conversation away from the subject of children, at least till after dinner.

And then, after the coffee, when Neville is serving liqueurs, that will be my chance. I'll just quietly get Mr. Brewster off by himself—into the library—and I'll tell him about my book. Then I'll give him the manuscript and ask him to publish it. I just know he'll be happy to do it. After all, isn't that what friends are for?

And why shouldn't he be happy to have it? I mean, it's not just an ordinary cookbook. I'm sure there can't possibly be another like it—so many wonderful stories from all the countries where Neville was posted—Austria, Malaysia, Argentina—mixed right in with marvelous recipes from Mama and Nanna Lloyd—handed down for generations—and all the wonderful cooks I've had—

Thursday, April 1

I'm so excited, I can't wait for tomorrow to come! I've asked Jean-Claude to do his wonderful salmon mousse for dinner tomorrow. And a good Chablis to go with it. What do you think, dear diary—would it be de trop to serve that wonderful Les Preuses we picked up in Burgundy on our last trip? 1970 was <u>such</u> a good year for Burgundy whites. And this <u>is</u> a very special occasion! Or is that putting it on a bit thick? Well, I'll leave that up to Neville, the wine is his department—he's so much more sensitive than I am about such matters.

So, the mousse and a Chablis. That, and a salad—greens only, I think—with Jean-Claude's lovely vinaigrette—he does it so well, with just a hint of dried curry—just the barest hint—don't want to over-whelm the mousse. And a dacquoise for dessert—absolutely my favorite! I'll leave the rest of the menu up to Jean-Claude—but he must make those darling little Austrian dinner rolls.—no one in New York can touch him when it comes to breads—

And then, when we have his tummy well-pampered, Llewellyn Brewster should be in a properly benign and receptive mood. N'est-ce pas, dear diary? Oh, my dear! I can't wait! This is so exciting!

Friday, April 2, 1999—A <u>most</u> special day!

My little cockleshell has been set on its way out into the big world! I am so excited, I can barely write these words.

Llewellyn has taken my precious manuscript!

The dear man—he was so surprised—
there he was, liqueur in one hand and my
heavy tome—almost 400 pages, for goodness' sake—in the other! Let me tell you all
about it, my dear, dear diary.

I waited until after dinner—which was
perfect, by the way!—the Les Preuses was
awfully good, with that very faint flintiness,
just right with the mousse, dear Neville
always chooses so well!—and I let everyone get settled down with their liqueurs.
Mimsy was just bursting to tell us about
some new marvel her darlings had
performed—teething, I think (what in the
world is so remarkable about a couple of
teeth showing up in babies' gums—they all
do it, don't they?)—and I knew that was my
perfect opportunity to rescue Llewellyn, so
I drew him away from the others into
Neville's library, sat him comfortably in
Neville's leather chair and then proceeded
to charm him with the history of the Lloyd
women—wonderful cooks, every one of
them. What incredible lives they had!—
pioneer women—and talented artists, too
(though none of them ever achieved
fame—unappreciated in their time, I'm
sure!)—and all beauties!—and of course, I

included myself, who has been fortunate enough to have lived all over the world—and Llewellyn was most kind—a dear man—though perhaps he was a bit fuddled by the wine. He took my manuscript and said he'd be sure to read it.

Oh, my dear, dear diary. It will be so exciting to see my book in print—I must be sure to send a signed copy to the Chadwicke Club, for the library. Roselynn Wyatt will be livid!—oh, là!—poor thing, now she won't be the only member with a published book to her credit—such trash she writes, anyway—do her good to have a little competition—

I can't <u>wait</u> for Llewellyn's call!

Monday, April 12

No word from Llewellyn yet. How long can it <u>take</u> the man to read one itty-bitty little book? Really!

Friday, April 16

Another week has passed and LB still has not called me. I've tried to catch him in the hall, but he seems to have vanished! I know they're not at their country place. I was leaving for the Philharmonic concert this afternoon, just as young Mackenzie was coming home from school. Well, as casually as I could, I asked if his mama and papa were away, but he said no and I couldn't very well pry, could I? So I just had to get into the elevator and leave him—I suppose to his milk and cookies. Nice young man. Nice manners.

Friday, April 23

One can't clutch at people, of course—but really, you'd think he'd have been in touch with me by now—could I be blamed if I just dropped him a note, do you think? But no, I mustn't press, it wouldn't do. But really!—the man must read as slowly as a dim-witted second-grader. I can't think how such a slow reader can be in the publishing business. But they do say it's a very reputable house—one of the oldest in New York. And his father was a member of the Cortlandt Club, so he must be all right. But really, my dear diary, this waiting is so hard. I am chewing my nails up to the elbow.

Which reminds me—did SherriLynn remember to schedule my manicure? I must call her.

Saturday, April 24

Still no word.

Sunday, April 25

Dreary Sunday. Maybe I shouldn't expect any word on the weekend.

Monday, April 26

Still no response from Llewellyn. This waiting will kill me!

April 27

Oh, my dear, dear, dear diary. I am devastated!!! I just can't believe—how could he? After eating at my table!!!! After drinking Neville's beautiful Chablis!!! I'm so angry, I could spit!!!!! No, I'm so angry—I can't think what I could do!

My manuscript was returned today. It came in the mail and I was so excited, I didn't even open the package at first. My heart was pounding and I had to have Louise bring me a cup of tea first, here in my sitting room. I locked my door. I drank my tea. I did a couple of Dr. Gupta's meditation exercises. (A fat lot of good it did me!) And then I opened the package.

There was only the briefest of cover letters and I will copy it here exactly. It said: "Henrietta, I'm returning your manuscript. We don't do this sort of book. Perhaps you would find a better home for it at one of the other publishers. I wish you good luck with it. Llewellyn Brewster."

How dare he!!? No more than those few pitiful, mealy-mouthed, spineless words. And not one of them tells me he even read my book. Not a single word about all the wonderful stories—didn't even notice the wonderful section on that time the Embassy was taken over by terrorists and Neville was held hostage for seventeen days until we sent in a rescue plan hidden in my famous terrine de canard. Wouldn't you think Llewellyn would be just dying to publish a book like that? Full of such stories! And every one of them true!

The nerve of the man! How dare he! How dare he eat at my table and refuse my book?!!!

I've spent the whole afternoon crying. Whatever shall I say to Neville when he comes home tonight? I look a fright. I shall have to call SherriLynn to do something with my face before 6:00.

Oh, my dear diary, I swear I shall never forgive Llewellyn Brewster as long as I live! Never! I mean it—I swear—I shall never again speak to him—not to him, not to his wife—not ever to any of them. Never!! Never!!!!!

# Chapter Fifteen

The diary fell out of Bridey's hands and slid down her lap and onto the floor. If she had been struck by lightning, the effect couldn't have been any more electrifying.

"So there was nothing more to it than that."

Her voice was a whisper in the silent room.

"The whole crazy feud was simply because Mack's father rejected Henrietta's book. Wait till I tell him. It was nothing more than that."

Silk climbed into her lap, and Bridey stroked her fur absentmindedly while her thoughts returned to the diary.

"How foolish Henrietta was to be so angry just because her book wasn't accepted by the first publisher she gave it to. Why, she was lucky he even looked at it, wasn't she, Silk?"

Silk stuck out a tiny pink tongue and licked a paw, apparently agreeing.

"She should have known better. A book often has to go to several publishers before it gets accepted.

Surely she knew that. And if she'd done just a little bit of checking before she approached him, she'd have found out his firm didn't publish cookbooks.

"But then, to have carried a grudge that way, to the grave. Even beyond the grave. To have caused so much trouble, and for such a silly, vain, high-handed reason."

She picked up the diary again and reread those last words.

I swear—I shall never again speak to him—not to him, not to his wife—not ever to any of them. Never!! Never!!!!!

"Did she think Llewellyn Brewster owed it to her to publish her book? Just because he was her neighbor and had eaten at her table? Just because she was accustomed to a life of indulgence and privilege and special favors. And then, did she not even try to talk to him about it?"

But Bridey already knew the answer to that question. As headstrong and stubborn and self-centered as Henrietta Willey was, once her mind was made up, there would have been no further discussion.

"Oh, I can't wait till Mack hears about this."

She felt a tingle in her cheeks and across the bridge of her nose, a little like the feeling she got when the vinegar in a salad dressing was too strong.

"Of course, that means confessing that I read Henrietta's diary. Do you think he'll be scandalized?"

Silk snuggled into Bridey's lap, and Bridey took that for reassurance. Silk would have done the same thing, for sure.

Now she was glad she'd agreed to see him again. Really glad.

"I brought the cats along. Will that be all right?"

She had arrived right on time, bearing a bowl of crispy hot French fries.

"Of course," Mack said. He was struggling to hang on to a bottle of wine and two glasses in one hand as he held the door for her with the other. "I was expecting them. Come on in."

She was bursting to tell him her news, but she was determined to wait for the right moment, and the effort added an extra measure of excitement to her usually lively manner. Mack had been expecting her to be cool and cautious, but instead he saw the heightened sparkle in her green eyes and the charming flush in her cheeks, the air of animation that danced all around her. In her bright miniskirt and skimpy little top, her slim form seemed especially fragile and feminine, and he felt his heart make a hot thump in his chest. The spicy fragrance of her hair distracted him as she passed him, entering the foyer of his apartment, and made a cloud of confusion in his head. For a moment he forgot the glasses in his hand, and it wasn't until she held up the bowl of fries and said, "Where do you want me to put these?" that he remembered why she was there.

"Oh," he said, recovering his wits and waving the glasses and the wine vaguely. "Outside, on the terrace."

He led her to the terrace, where the table was already set in a bizarre mixture of picnic casual and banquet formal. The tablecloth was the traditional red-and-white check, but the napkins were fancy double damask. The silver was hand wrought, the plates were paper. The buns were still in their cellophane wrap, but next to them was a crystal bowl filled with ketchup. A tiny, rose-patterned silver ladle stuck up out of the ketchup, its ornate design gleaming in the late afternoon light that bathed the terrace in gold as the sun dropped over the Hudson River.

Bridey laughed at the odd display.

"I was torn," Mack said. "I couldn't decide whether to make this an informal barbecue or go all out to impress you. Seems I got stuck some-where in between."

He already had a platter of raw burgers ready to be grilled, including some tiny ones for the cats, and after offering her a choice of beer, Coke or wine—she chose the wine—he was ready to start them going. She set the bowl of fries on the table. Dishes for Silk and Satin were waiting next to

Scout's, and the two cats did their usual cat thing, examining every corner of the terrace for potential hiding places, while Scout watched them eagerly, like a proud host happy to show off his home to new visitors. He'd never had guests of his own before and was on his very best behavior.

"They seem to be getting along pretty well, don't you think?" Mack said as he prepared to cook the hamburgers.

"Like old friends."

"And how do they like their hamburgers," Mack asked, "rare, medium or well done?"

"Medium rare."

"And you?"

"Very rare," she said.

"Me, too."

He laid the raw meat over the hottest part of the coals.

"I've got an apology to make," he said as he tended the burgers, which started to sizzle immediately, their aroma rising invitingly into the air. "I've been thinking about it all day. I shouldn't have teased you about letting Silk get out that night. It seemed kind of funny at the time, and it didn't take a lot of IQ points to figure out what was bouncing around in your bag. That and the look on your face: trying so hard to be cool and looking so scared at the same time."

"You're right about that. I was plenty scared."

"How did it happen?"

"I don't really know. She must have slipped into my bag when I wasn't looking and then slipped out again down at the fish market. I was there for almost an hour, and apparently she had herself a high old time during that time. The amazing thing is that she turned up just as I was ready to leave. It was such a coincidence. I looked up and there she was, cool as you please. She jumped into my bag like it was her taxi home. If I'd left the market a minute earlier, I'd have totally missed her. And what's even scarier, I wouldn't have realized till hours later that she wasn't in the apartment, and then she could have been gone for good. I wouldn't have had a clue where to look for her."

"Are you always so lucky?"

Bridey laughed. "My grandma used to say I carry a guardian angel on my shoulder. And I certainly did that time. But I've been feeling guilty ever since, and I hated having to lie to Mr. Kinski about it."

"You feel better now that the secret's out?"

"I sure do." She lifted her glass in a kind of toast and said, "I have to thank you for not giving me away." And then, as he raised his spatula in acknowledgment, she added, "I know another secret."

"Oh?"

"Mmmm." She savored the moment. "It concerns you. And it's a biggie."

He looked at her thoughtfully. "A real biggie?"

"Oh, you bet!"

He put the burgers into the buns, slipped them onto the plates and brought them to the table.

"Maybe I'd better sit down."

"Maybe you'd better."

She smiled knowingly at him, looking disarmingly nonchalant and drawing out the moment as long as she could.

"I'm sitting," he said.

She carefully spooned some ketchup out of the crystal bowl and dropped it in globs on her hamburger. She laid a slice of raw onion over that and covered it all up with the toasted bun top. Then she reconsidered, removed the onion and set it at the edge of her plate.

*You never know . . .*

She laughed to herself as she noticed that Mack was doing the same thing.

"Okay," he said at last, preparing to take a bite of his hamburger. "I'm ready."

"I found out why Henrietta Willey was so mad at your family."

Mack paused with his hamburger in midair. His mouth, opened to receive it, had forgotten its job and remained agape, making him look a little foolish, and he stayed that way while she told him about her discovery of the diary and its revelations. Many heartbeats passed as he took in the full significance of her news. Then he replaced his burger on his plate and closed his mouth.

"I don't believe this," he said incredulously.

"Well, believe it."

"You mean to tell me that all those years, all that insane hostility of hers was based on nothing more than my father's rejection of her cookbook? That's crazy!"

He got up and walked over to the edge of the terrace and looked down for a minute. Then he raised his eyes, as though to heaven, turned back to Bridey and lifted his hands in a gesture of exasperation.

"We don't even publish cookbooks. Surely she must have understood that."

"Well, your father's note was a little brusque. Maybe if he'd been a little more tactful—spoken to her personally . . ."

"Nonsense! She was just a spoiled, self-centered woman. Expecting to have her hand held, thinking the world owed her favors—"

"That's a little harsh, don't you think?" Bridey found herself rising to Henrietta's defense. "She was a first-time author and she'd put her heart and soul into her manuscript. That's a very vulnerable experience, something totally new for someone like Henrietta. Surely your father had dealt with enough writers to have understood that. And he could have told her right off that it wasn't his kind of book without putting her through weeks of suspense. He must have known what torture the waiting would be for a writer. I think it was heartless of him."

Mack's dark eyes flashed angrily. "You can't talk about my father that way. You didn't even know him. And what makes you think writers need such coddling? Writers are accustomed to rejection. That's part of the writing game. And anyway, no offense, Bridey, but cookbooks just aren't in the same class as the kind of work we handle at Harmon and Brewster. If Henrietta had done her homework, she would have known we publish serious, scholarly nonfiction. You would know that, wouldn't you? You wouldn't ask me, for example, to publish your book. I'm sure it's a fine book and all that, and cookbooks serve a valid purpose, I suppose, but after all, we do have very high standards."

"Oh! So cookbooks don't meet your precious 'standards.' Is that it? And that justifies being rude and unkind to an old woman who'd worked hard to produce something she thought had some value."

"Now, wait a minute. You're making her sound like a wispy, little old apple-cheeked grandma," Mack interrupted her impatiently. "Henrietta Willey was tough as nails and hard as tempered steel. Her trouble was, she expected everyone to cater to her, and when she didn't get special treatment, she turned into a viper. And my father wasn't rude or unkind to her. He just sent her a nice little note that didn't happen to say what she wanted to hear. That's not a crime, you know."

"Well . . ."

"I'd probably have done the same thing myself. I *do* do the same thing myself. All the time. Harmon and Brewster has to reject most of what's submitted to us. Though usually it's our editors who do the rejecting. Actually, my father did her the courtesy of writing to her himself."

"Oh, big deal!"

Mack was struggling with his rising temper. What did this girl know about the publishing business? How could she possibly understand the pressures: of time, of market demands, of bottom lines?

But still . . .

He came back to the table, sat down and looked seriously at her for a long minute. His eyes searched hers, and what he saw in them were her stubbornness and her passionate commitment to her own dreams, striking contrasts to her hair, made more golden than ever in the sunset, and the soft, feminine grace of her delicate shoulders and slim, shapely arms. His gaze dropped to her hands, with their little nicks and burns and bruises. Perhaps it was the air of brave strength that he saw in her fine features, the tiny, harsh signs of her work that showed on her lovely hands. He felt again that surge of protectiveness, like a sudden rein on his anger. His loyalty to his father made him ready to do battle in his name, but he realized he couldn't bear to be unkind to this girl.

"Bridey." He spoke with unaccustomed restraint. "I understand how you might be sympathetic to

Henrietta's efforts, even if she was a wicked old bat—"

"She wasn't a wicked old bat!"

"She was too. She was a bad-tempered, vindictive woman. And maybe, because she shared your passion for cooking and wrote about it, just as you do, you feel a kind of kinship with her. But still, my father did the right thing, and I'm surprised to hear you attack him. As I said, I'm sure I would have done the same thing myself."

"Oh, you would, would you?"

"Yes, I would." His voice carried an air of finality, as though the matter was closed.

But Bridey had to have the last word. "Well, you'd be wrong."

After that there seemed to be nothing left to say. Mack's long habit of siding with his father stopped his mouth, leaving him rigidly defensive. He felt as though he'd painted himself into a corner, asserting his father's rectitude even when he knew what a tactless curmudgeon the old man could be. And Bridey, though incensed at Mack's apparent cold-heartedness, felt foolish for having defended a silly, demanding old woman. Both of them had been left unable to find any reasonable topic of discussion.

So they ate their hamburgers in silence and frustration, each one stuck in a hole of their own digging.

And yet, even as they struggled with the stubbornness that sat like an iron fence separating them, something—perhaps it was the last radiance of the setting sun—blanketed them, creating a current of warmth that seemed to leap the space between them. Though Mack's jaw was set in a mask of manly resolve, and he was determined to remain unmoved, his heart ached, telling him to reach across the table and take her hand in his. The shine of her hair in the soft light begged to be touched. The long fringe of her lashes, lowered while she ate—for she refused to raise her eyes to look at him—was heart-stoppingly lovely, and he yearned to feel them brushing his lips.

Absentmindedly, he picked French fries from the bowl, slogging them around in the puddle of ketchup on his plate and eating them slowly, then licking his fingers—just the way his mother had taught him not to.

Bridey, too, felt the strange current. It seemed to run up her arms and down her spine, down and down, all the way to her toes, and she feared she was going to faint again. She wanted to reach across the table, right across the bowl of ketchup and the plate of sliced onion, to touch his hair, to run her fingers through it, to trace with her fingertips the black brows, the strong bones of his face, the curve of his lips . . .

But they continued to eat in silence.

And when they were finished, and she automatically offered to help clean up, his "No, thanks, I can handle it" was abrupt.

"Fine," she said. And she was out of the apartment, with Silk and Satin scooting along quickly to keep up with her.

Mack was left staring at the door.

"Scout," he said, "I was right, wasn't I?"

The dog walked out of the room in exasperation.

And back in her own apartment, Bridey dropped disconsolately onto the sofa and held Silk close to her for comfort.

"Oh, he is so stubborn! He just hasn't a clue how wrong he is. Has he, Silk?"

Silk refused to respond, and Bridey decided she must be agreeing with her.

"But you know, Mack was right about one thing. Henrietta's dream was exactly the same as mine. It's almost spooky. Of all the people who might have wound up here in this apartment, taking care of you and Satin, isn't it strange that it turned out to be me? Like it's magic or something. Because, just like her, I'm creating a cookbook out of a family's history, using recipes and stories that have been collected over generations. Do you suppose it means something?"

Silk just snuggled into her lap, and Bridey was left alone with her musings, which quickly drifted from Henrietta and cookbooks to thoughts of a certain strong jaw and waves of dark hair, a tall, handsome shape in chinos and a light blue oxford shirt, and a cheery wave of a spatula. . . .

# Chapter Sixteen

Mack was at his desk, brooding. He'd been glowering for days now, snarling impatiently at everyone who came near, and this morning had brought no improvement in his foul mood. Helen and the rest of his staff continued to stay nervously out of his way, waiting for the storm to blow over.

Finally, after trying without any success to attend to the pile of work on his desk, he gave up in angry frustration and tossed his pen down on the papers in front of him. He punched a key on the intercom.

"Helen?" His voice came through the phone with the peremptory bark of an angry drill sergeant.

"Yes, Mr. Brewster?" Helen kept her tone as neutral as she could, but she braced herself, sitting up a little straighter than usual. She made a face at Janet Warensky, whose smile was sympathetic as she laid the morning sales reports on Helen's desk.

"Helen, I want you to go back in the files and locate anything you have on a manuscript submitted by a Mrs. Henrietta Willey. That's W-I-L-L-E-Y. It would be some time in the spring of 1999. There should be a letter to Mrs. Willey from my father, and I especially want to see that. It should be in the files for April or early May of that year. Get it all to me as soon as you have it."

"That'll be in the archives, Mr. Brewster," she

said cautiously, afraid of eliciting an eruption. "It's going to take a while."

"Then get on it right away, dammit!"

He punched the button again, cutting her off.

Then he sat there at his desk for a long time, glaring at the large portrait of his father, which glared back at him from the opposite wall.

He didn't like the way he was feeling: angry and guilty and defensive. Like something explosive was bottled up inside him. And whatever it was, it was something important, something he couldn't ignore. Mack was a man of action and command; it was impossible for him to sit quietly. But now he was completely stymied. He had to do something, but he hadn't a clue what it was. He tugged at his tie, loosening it. He ran his hands through his hair, messing it up. He got up and paced the room several times. He sat down again, shuffled helplessly through the papers on his desk, and then gave up trying to concentrate on the work in front of him. This thing, whatever it was, was making him nuts.

Downtown, at the New York Surrogate's Court, Afton Morley's kinship hearing was about to start. The referee, Gilbert Forsgren, sat at a desk to one side of the room, facing a long conference table around which were gathered all the interested parties. Afton and Mulie were there, on one side of the table, with their lawyer, Bryan Chubb. Opposite them, on the other side of the table, Gerald Kinski sat with his hands folded, waiting for the referee to begin the proceedings. Next to Gerald were Alan Grossman, appointed as guardian ad litem "for persons unknown," Charles Chessler, representing the office of the County Public Administrator and Harold Maudsley, for the co-op board. All the lawyers were dressed in dark gray, as though that were the uniform of the day, and on the floor next to each was a bulging briefcase. A microphone was set before each person, connected to a digital recorder.

Bridey was there, too. Gerry Kinski had invited her to observe and, with the referee's permission, she'd been offered a seat apart from the others, facing the end of the table. Her nerves were on edge, with her whole life riding on the outcome of this hearing, and she had to force herself to maintain a composed and professional air of detachment. Though she hadn't slept well and hadn't been able to eat any breakfast, she was determined to show a quiet and respectful demeanor. Her knees felt shaky, and she was glad she didn't have to participate in any way, for she wouldn't have trusted herself to keep up her pose of objectivity. She was wearing her very nicest business-type suit, and the russet color of the soft, nubby fabric and the creamy silk of her blouse set off her coppery hair beautifully, giving an extra glow to her eyes. Behind her was an enormous window that reached high above her head toward the distant ceiling, and though it was layered with accumulated city grime and dust, it let in a shaft of filtered morning light that fell across her, softening the harsh fluorescence coming from the fixtures set into the ceiling. From her position at the end of the room, she was able to observe all the participants, and she made a quick inventory of everyone seated at the table.

First there was Mulie, who was plainly nervous. Though she kept her feet firmly on the floor and set tight together, she kept shifting her plump bottom back and forth on her seat, as though it was too small for her. Her hands were in constant motion, patting at the little curls that surrounded her face and pulling at her skirt, which kept riding up over her knees, and she avoided the eyes of everyone in the room while glancing repeatedly at the microphone in front of her, as though she expected it to bite her. She had dressed up for the occasion in a lavender polyester suit that bunched up at the back, and for the hundredth time since arriving in New York she promised herself that she really would go on a diet, as soon as she returned to Twin Falls. She fiddled nervously with a mass of papers she had drawn out of her copious straw bag, removing paper clips and putting them back on again, leafing through them repeatedly as though to assure herself that nothing was missing.

Afton was leaning back in his chair, his jacket

open and falling back from a checked shirt that strained at its buttons and bulged over his belt buckle. Unlike Mulie, he seemed totally at ease, and never once, through the whole proceedings, did he remove his hat. He was apparently entirely assured of the outcome of this proceeding, and his smugly relaxed posture, backed up by the imposing pile of documents in Mulie's hands, only added to Bridey's worries.

The Morleys' lawyer, Bryan Chubb, was the very picture of his name, being a short, portly man with multiple chins and round red cheeks upon which his glasses, also round, rode primly. He wore a dark gray suit, highly polished black shoes and a dark tie. He had the happily confident air of a man whose clients were about to become very wealthy.

The lawyers facing the Morley side, Gerry and the others, chatted amiably among themselves, catching up on their news and sharing anecdotes while they waited for the hearing to begin.

Mr. Forsgren, the referee, was a tidy man, with long, delicate hands and a graceful manner. He was dressed conservatively in a dark blue suit and a striped tie, and his voice, when he spoke, had a faintly Jamaican lilt. He opened the manila file folder in front of him, scanned its first page briefly, then said, "All right, then. Are we ready?" When everyone nodded, he punched the play button to start recording.

"This is case number thirteen-one-o-seven," he

dictated mechanically, as one who has done this same thing a thousand times, "in the matter of Afton Morley, claimant to the estate of Henrietta Willey." He recorded the names of those present with their titles and affiliations, including Bridey, whose observer status was duly noted. And then, "Mr. Chubb, will you please proceed?"

Mr. Chubb took several packets of paper from his briefcase and handed them out to each of the attorneys. While each man unfolded what appeared to be an extraordinarily long length of paper, too long to spread out in its entirety, he passed another copy to Bridey.

"In case you'd like to follow along," he said.

Bridey had never seen anything like this document. There wasn't room enough on her lap to open it completely, but she was able to extend it sufficiently to see that it was a family tree, drawn horizontally across the page. A profusion of printed boxes, each almost two inches square, filled the paper, and black lines were drawn between the boxes to indicate spouses and offspring. Each box contained the name of a single individual and their relevant birth, marriage and death dates. Spread out, the whole sheet was about seven feet long, but Bridey had room across her lap for only three or four segments. The name *Lloyd* appeared frequently in the little boxes.

"This," said Mr. Chubb, speaking for the record, "is the family tree of Afton Lloyd Morley and delineates his status as first cousin twice removed of the decedent, Henrietta Lloyd Caswell Willey." His voice was flat, without emotion. He, too, had taken part in hearings like this a thousand times.

Afton smiled complacently and Mulie pursed her lips, as though daring anyone to challenge her husband's claim. They were the picture of smug anticipation, and Bridey felt like smacking them.

Mr. Chubb handed another sheaf of documents to the referee and said, "Mrs. Morley has gathered this material in support of my client's claim. With your permission, I'll let her explain each document as we trace Mr. Morley's kinship on the family tree."

"That'll be fine," said the referee. "Go ahead, Mrs. Morley."

With Chubb's help, Mulie opened the paper to its full length, stretching it to the end of the table. The lawyer and Afton both moved back their chairs to give her the room she needed as she moved back and forth, using the family tree to illustrate her explanation. Her voice shook a bit at first, and she tugged awkwardly at the back of her jacket several times, pulling it down over her round bottom, but she gathered confidence as she went along, for this was a subject on which she was prepared. In a few minutes her voice and her trembling hands stopped shaking and she seemed to forget her nerves as she discussed each little box on the family tree in turn, tracing the history of the Lloyd clan.

"Now, this here's Josiah Lloyd, Afton's grand-father," she began, resting her plump index finger on the box at the very top of the sheet. "That paper you're holding," she indicated the yellow document with a bright green seal that Mr. Forsgren was reading, "that's an extract from the church records, and it shows Josiah was born on March 17, 1866." She waited a moment while Mr. Forsgren read the document and marked it as Exhibit A.

"Now, in January 1884, when he was almost eighteen years old, Josiah married Lydia Mack." Mulie's finger moved to the box next to Josiah's. "You have the record of his marriage there, next one in the pile. That was back in the territorial days, before Idaho was admitted to the Union, and the only records they had back then were kept by the church elders."

Mr. Forsgren set aside Josiah's birth certificate and carefully picked up the next item in the pile, a frayed, fragile bit of paper attesting to the marriage of Josiah Lloyd and Lydia Mack. He noted that Lydia's wedding date was also the date of her sixteenth birthday.

"We found that in an old family Bible," Mulie said. "I'd appreciate your being real careful with it, Your Honor, because it's already falling to pieces and it's kind of like a family heirloom."

"Of course, Mrs. Morley. We're accustomed to handling delicate old documents here. I'll have my clerk place it in a plastic cover for safekeeping."

Mulie sniffed, as though she wasn't so sure he'd be up to the job.

"So, like you can see there," she continued, "Lydia was sixteen when they married—you got papers for her, too, in there. Now, here's the fourteen children they had." Her finger touched each box in the next row down. "Of the fourteen, only two actually survived. The first was Jason Lloyd, the oldest child; he was born in December 1884, just short of Lydia's seventeenth birthday. And this here," her finger ran along the row to its last box, "this here's the other, the youngest, Patience Lloyd, born in 1910. And Patience Lloyd was Afton's mother."

Bridey was doing the calculations in her head. She had tried to follow along on her copy of the tree, unfolding it enough to view a portion of it at a time, but found it too cumbersome to manage. Finally she just folded it back up and determined to examine it more closely later on. Despite Mulie's matter-of-fact comments, Bridey had seen enough of the information printed in the little boxes to be struck by the extraordinary real-life dramas that were hidden there. Poor old Lydia Lloyd, for example, married at sixteen, had had fourteen children over the next twenty-six years, and had lost almost all of them; three of them in one year. What dreadful accidents, illnesses or epidemics had carried them off? And she had been forty-two years old when her last child was born. Why, even with today's modern technology, a pregnancy at that age could mean serious problems. In Lydia's time it would truly have been a life-and-death risk. Bridey was awed by the courage of those pioneer women, and for the moment her own anxieties seemed trivial.

Mulie went on. "Now Jason, here," she said, her finger moving down the line, "he married an older woman. Martha Hansen, right here, born in 1874. She was twenty-eight when her first husband, Heber, died, and she already had four little ones. Jason was only eighteen himself, but he adopted them all, gave them his name, Lloyd, and it was the oldest one, Henry—that was Henrietta Willey's grandfather—he was twelve years old when Martha and Jason got married, in 1902. You got all the papers for each one of them, there in the pile."

Afton spoke up for the first time. "My lawyer here," he said with an air of challenge in his voice, "Mr. Chubb, he tells me adopted kids count just as much as natural-born ones, isn't that right?"

"It certainly is," Mr. Forsgren assured him. "Adopted children and half siblings and children born outside of a legal marriage, too. They all count in establishing consanguinity. That is, the degree of kinship."

"I know what consanguinity means." Afton said the unfamiliar word slowly, taking care with each syllable. His face looked belligerent, as though he dared anyone to put him down. "Mr. Chubb here explained it to me."

"Of course, Mr. Morley." Mr. Forsgren's tone was conciliatory.

"And first cousins, once removed, twice removed, even three times removed, that doesn't matter either, isn't that right? They're all entitled?"

"Absolutely, Mr. Morley. In New York State, a first cousin no matter how distant, is entitled to assert a claim."

Afton relaxed, apparently satisfied. His lawyer pursed his plump lips in irritation. Hadn't his client believed what he'd told him?

"Lucky for me they kept having all those kids," Afton observed coolly, "spitting 'em out like peanuts. And lucky for me old Mulie here's kept up with all her genealogy work. She's done a great job putting this all together."

"Yes, indeed, Mr. Morley."

Mulie blushed right up to her frizzed, faded hair. To hide her embarrassment, she went on quickly with her explanation.

"Now, over here," she continued, "this here's Afton's line." Her finger rested again on the box headed PATIENCE LLOYD.

"This was Afton's mother," she said. "She was born in 1910 and she didn't marry till she was thirty-eight. That's when she married Theron Morley, Afton's father, in 1948, but she and Theron didn't have Afton until 1952, when she was forty-two. Forty-two years old, just like her mother was when she was born. Theron was eleven years older than Patience, so he was fifty-three when Afton was born. And Afton here was their only child."

Again, Bridey found herself imagining the drama that lay hidden in the family tree's seemingly inarticulate combinations of little boxes: a late marriage for Patience to a considerably older Theron, two aging parents bringing up a single child. Her lively mind was spinning out a variety of domestic scenarios to explain Afton's defensively sour, domineering temperament.

Mulie's finger moved back inexorably to Jason's line.

"Now see, back here, over on Jason's side, he and Martha Hansen had a bunch of kids of their own, but the only one of the whole bunch that survived was Jason's adopted boy, Henry, who married Catherine Morton in 1910. They had two girls and it was the older one, Emily, born in 1911, who married Marshall Caswell in 1928, when she was seventeen."

Here, Mulie's finger moved down to the bottom row, to a single box that was larger than all the others and outlined thickly in black ink.

"And in 1929," she said, with an air of triumph at having come to the end of the line, "they had their only child, a daughter. And that was Henrietta Lloyd Caswell, who married Neville Willey."

All the eyes in the room fixed on that one large box, with Henrietta Willey's name in it. The source of all this trouble. Bridey's heart sank. It was all so irrefutable. The documents were apparently authentic. Mulie's research was faultless. The conclusion was inevitable. Bridey Berrigan's dreams were toast.

"So," Mulie went on, her finger running back up the series of boxes and lines and then returning down on the other side, "if you trace it on back, through Jason's line to Josiah and then back down through Patience, you can see that Afton was Henrietta's first cousin twice removed, that we never even knew about till we saw that piece in the *Times-News*."

She looked around the room with a self-satisfied expression that said plainly, *See! I told you so!* Then she returned to her chair and perched on its edge, proud to have delivered the results of her diligent genealogical research. From here on, the questions and answers would be handled by Mr. Chubb, and she could relax.

And Bridey felt her future cracking apart in little pieces, falling down around her feet in a little heap on the hearing-room floor. It was back to hot kitchens and hundred-pound sacks of potatoes. For sure.

Mack Brewster paced his office. He stared out of the window. He tried to concentrate on his correspondence and kept losing track of what was in front of him. Helen was still hunting through the archives, and Mack's impatience was boiling up to his teeth. But it wasn't the Willey file that was driving him nuts. That was just an excuse, and he knew it.

It was his father, staring down at him from the wall. And it was Bridey and everything she had said that night. And the two of them were crashing against each other, the slim little sprite of a girl taking on the formidable and indomitable Llewellyn Brewster. Mack's head felt like a war was going on inside it. First he told himself she just didn't understand. He told himself she was wrong. He told himself she was prejudiced by her own self-interest. But then a montage of images played through his brain, like a movie: Bridey on his terrace, with the breeze blowing through her hair and the sun filling the delicate curls with gold; Bridey jogging through the park, damp and glowing from the exercise, or sitting on a rock, licking a Popsicle like a little girl; Bridey curled up on the sofa, with the cats soft and quiet, close to her; Bridey stirring a pot of goulash, the aromatic vapors steaming up around her . . .

"Oh, the hell with this!" he said suddenly, furious with himself. "I've got to get out of here!"

He slammed out of his office and headed for the park. If he didn't walk, he'd go crazy.

And at that very moment, Gilbert Forsgren was dictating the last remarks into the machine.

"Having heard the testimony of the parties and having received documents provided by the claimant together with all submissions by counsel, the court will review all the evidence and motions and will render its decision at a future date."

He looked around, as though to be sure there were no further comments. Then he said with great finality, "This hearing is now closed."

And he hit the stop button.

# Chapter Seventeen

"Stop playing with your food," Marge said. "You're making me nervous."

"Oh, Marge, I'm just too miserable to eat."

They'd met for lunch at Gilligan's Pub, famous for steaks so enormous, a single T-bone could feed a village in India for a month. Bridey had ordered only a salad, and even that seemed to her unappealing. She was hardly touching it, just pushing the arugula leaves and fresh basil around on her plate and making a little mound of tomato slices and mushroom bits in the center of the greens.

"You're so lucky," Marge said enviously. "When I feel rotten, I eat a carton of Häagen-Dazs."

"You want to see luck, you go look at the Morleys. Can you believe those two? Now there's real luck for you." Bridey grimaced disdainfully. "It looks like Afton and Mulie are going to take over the whole estate." She nibbled mournfully on a roll. "Mulie!" She spoke the name as though she'd bitten into an unripe persimmon. "Can you imagine anyone standing still for a name like that? I'd throw a frying pan at my husband if he tried to stick a label like that on me."

"Tell me about it," Marge said. Then she laughed. "No, I mean, really. Tell me about the hearing. How did it go? What happened?"

So Bridey described the events of the morning. "Mulie had done a ton of research and she had this big stack of documents all lined up like ducks in a row. I'm no expert, but it all looked pretty authentic to me. If everything checks out, they're going to get it all. And there won't be a thing the co-op board or Mack Brewster can do about it. And as for me, I'll be out on my ear, along with the poor cats."

"And to think," Marge said, commiserating, "all of this might never have happened if Mack's father hadn't rejected Henrietta's book."

"Or at least," Bridey added, "if he hadn't done it in such a thoughtless, inconsiderate way. The whole dumb feud might never have started if Mr. Brewster had used just a little care, just a smidge of tact."

"You know, Bridey," Marge said thoughtfully, "I've been thinking about that manuscript. From what you described, it sounds like the kind of thing we'd have been interested in at *Lady Fair*. It would have made a wonderful serial for us. Do you have any idea what happened to it?"

"Not a clue. I assume Mrs. Willey was so discouraged by the whole experience, she just got rid of it. Probably burned it up in a fit of pique. Or rage, more like it."

"But maybe not," Marge said slowly. Her editor's nose was twitching, and her imagination had been stirred by the idea of generations of creative domestic effort handed down from mother to daughter, embellished by world travel, a sophisticated palate and lots of money, eventually finding its expression in a glamorous setting. She was getting more interested every moment, and her enthusiasm gathered steam with each word. "I don't think she'd have burned it up. I don't think she'd have been able to get rid of it at all, not after she'd put so much love and work into it. If you ask me, I'd bet she hid it away somewhere, right there in the apartment. Just like she did her diary."

"You think?" Bridey mulled over the idea and began to share Marge's fantasy. "You might be right, Marge. And wouldn't that be great? If we could find it?"

"Oh, I'd love it!" Marge was all animation now. She was waving her fingers in front of her face, fluttering her red nails like signal flags. "Why don't we do it? Why don't we hunt for it?"

"Well . . ."

"We could! I could come over tonight and we could have a treasure hunt, just you and me. We could order in pizzas and make popcorn. It would be like a slumber party!"

"Well . . ."

"Come on. It'll be fun. I'll bring a bottle of wine and we'll ransack the whole place, top to bottom. Just what you need to cheer you up."

"Well, I guess . . ."

"Good! That's settled, then. Seven o'clock tonight."

Meanwhile, in the park, Mack's demons had followed right along with him and would not be shaken loose; they stayed at his side, stride for stride, nagging at him furiously as he tried to sort out his feelings.

Loyalty was a matter of honor with Mack Brewster, as much a part of him as his wavy hair and his dark eyes. Obeying its commands was as habitual as brushing his teeth. And he would sooner have put his hand in a fire than let an outsider criticize his father.

But dammit, no one needed to tell him how domineering and inconsiderate his father could be. Hadn't he had to come up against that powerful personality day in and day out, every move he'd ever made? Hadn't he had to practically go to the mat with the old man dozens of times? Didn't he know better than anyone else how hard it was to have a father who always knew what was what? And—the hardest part of all—a father who was always right. Ever since he was a kid, he'd always been jumping back and forth between being proud of his father and being infuriated by him. The man had had a will of iron, and Mack had had to develop his own iron will to stand up to him.

Did she think it was easy, believing your dad was the best there was while always, at the same time, needing to shake loose of him?

*"She."*

There it was, like a pebble in his shoe, making him crazy.

He kicked at a loose stone and snarled at it as it skittered off into the bushes.

She!

How had *she* happened? What was it about this one? There'd been girls before, plenty of girls, but none of them had ever taken up residence in his head. Or in his heart.

Without a word of warning.

Just sailed into his life, with her coffee cakes and her stews and her sun-filled, cinnamon-scented hair and her lithe, little-girl look, and all of a sudden the habits of a lifetime had been shaken up like a bag of marbles, making him question the rules he'd lived by, the rules he'd been brought up to obey.

Why couldn't he brush it away, like a minor irritation not worthy of his attention? Somehow Bridey's challenge had turned his iron will to oatmeal and here he was, thinking the unthinkable.

The thought glowed in his head like a tiny, persistent flame: maybe his father really had behaved stupidly.

And maybe a lightning bolt would strike him down, right there on a path in Central Park.

Or . . . or maybe he was going to have to go to the mat with the old man one more time.

He looked around as though hoping to find a helping hand, or maybe a guardian angel. Nearby, a girl sat on a rock, eating an ice cream on a stick. She didn't even look like Bridey—her hair was dark, and she was short and a bit plump—but the sight of her triggered a memory. His heart twisted.

How did Bridey have the power to get inside him, change him, make him confront the veil he'd drawn over his father's memory, pull it away and look behind it?

He parked himself on a bench, wishing she were sitting there, next to him.

A little boy on a tricycle rode past, going *vroom, vroom* like an engine, pumping his little legs hard. Not far behind, an elderly gentleman, carrying his jacket over his arm, followed along. Obviously the child's grandfather.

That's what his father had wanted—to have his grandchildren gathered around him, living close by, playing in the park.

*You would have liked her, Dad. And you know what? She'd have been able to stand up to you. Not many girls could do that.*

The girl on the rock finished her ice cream and turned her face up to the sun, trying to get a few minutes' tanning time.

*What makes Bridey so different?*

Why couldn't he get her out of his head? Why was her approval so important to him? Why did displeasing her hurt so much? Why did her trouble cause him so much pain? What was going on? What was making his heart feel like it was being squeezed?

He looked at his watch.

*Maybe Helen has that file by now,* he thought. He got up from the bench and reluctantly, slowly, walked back to his office.


It wasn't much of a file. It lay open on his desk, its few pages spread out in front of him.

Mack read through it again.

There was a cover sheet, identifying the manuscript Henrietta had submitted, and the editor's note, dated April 29, 1980:

> An interesting slant, with some really good
> stories backing up the recipes—maybe the

other way around, the recipes backing up the tales of travel and the family memoir. And the Willey name might have some market value. The writing needs a lot of work; strictly amateur. And it would need a cooking editor, too. Additional $$$— photos, recipe testing, etc. Not for us. Want me to write to her?

Scrawled across the bottom, in his father's familiar broad hand, were the words *No. I'll take care of it.* It was signed with the initials *LB*, slanted forcefully across the bottom corner of the paper.

And the infamous letter, a copy of which had also been stored in Helen's file, was in Mack's hands.

Henrietta, I'm returning your manuscript. We don't do this sort of book. Perhaps you would find a better home for it at one of the other publishers. I wish you good luck with it. Llewellyn Brewster.

Mack read the letter several times. He could hear his father's peremptory voice dictating it; just another piece of work in a busy day. Mack knew his father would have given it no more than a moment's thought. Poor Henrietta!

Then a new idea slipped into the mix.

*Actually, we might have made something of it. It might have been of interest as a memoir, or maybe a social-historical piece. Hmmm. Could have been worth at least a second look. It would be interesting to see that manuscript. It certainly has caused enough trouble. Wonder what happened to it.*

He read the letter again. Maybe for the sixth time. He realized how dismissive it must have sounded to Henrietta. An experienced writer would be accustomed to curt rejection letters, but Henrietta wasn't an experienced writer. No matter how many countries she'd lived in, no matter how many famous people she'd known, as a writer she was just a beginner, and probably as timid as any twenty-year-old sending out a first manuscript. What's more, the world pampered people like Henrietta; it paid attention to their wishes and jumped to satisfy them. She'd have been totally unprepared—no, she'd have been really insulted— by being rejected so casually.

*Would it have been so hard, Dad? Just a little consideration, just a moment to write a few more words? You knew the woman; you'd been a guest in her home. You could have made it a touch more personal, written something a little encouraging instead of just brushing her off with a canned rejection. Maybe you could even have knocked on her door, spoken to her personally.*

But of course, that wouldn't have been his

father's way. Sentimental indulgence, he'd have called it. No time for that in a busy, demanding world. Who knew that better than his son?

Mack drummed his pencil on the desktop.

*Is that what Bridey will be facing when the time comes for her to try to get her book published? Is that what you would have done to her?*

He drummed some more. Then he dropped the pencil and closed the file. He'd made a decision.

*Dad, you and I are going to have a little talk.*

"Helen," he said into the intercom, "I'm leaving now. I have to take care of something. See you in the morning." Then he remembered to add, "And thanks for getting that file for me."

As he rode down in the elevator, he realized his heart was pounding.

# Chapter Eighteen

The living room was almost dark, but by some trick of reflected light the setting sun sent a single golden shaft through the partially drawn living room drapes, casting it across Henrietta's portrait and imparting a mysterious glow to her face.

Bridey stopped in her tracks. She put her hand on Marge's arm.

"What do you think, Marge? Is the old girl," she pointed to the picture, "is she okay with us prowling around through her things, looking for that manuscript?"

Marge paused only briefly. She tilted her head to one side and gave the painting a quick, appraising glance.

"I'd say it's the very thing she's been waiting for," Marge said matter-of-factly. "Like you were heaven-sent, Bridey: the exactly right person to dig that old manuscript of hers out of the moth-balls, or wherever it is she stashed it."

Marge wasn't interested in spending one more minute obsessing about ethical or mystical questions. She was already halfway into the next room. This promised to be the best adventure she'd had in ages and she was eager to get started. "Come on," she called back impatiently. "I know it's here somewhere. My editorial nose can smell a manuscript at twenty paces."

Bridey took one last look up at the picture. The shaft of light gave a spooky shine to the portrait's eyes, but it was impossible to tell if it was a spark of encouragement or a gleam of warning. Were she and Marge about to find hidden treasure, buried somewhere in the enormous apartment? Or were they more like reckless children, poking around and exploring where they had no business going, violating Henrietta's privacy?

But, like the little girl who'd been told not to put beans up her nose, she found the challenge irresistible.

"Whatever you do," she called, hurrying to join Marge, who was already in Neville's bedroom, "don't make a mess."

"Of course not," Marge said. "I'll be totally careful." She was already pulling the pillows forward and feeling behind them, probing under the mattress. "I'll just start in here and go through this room first. You do Henrietta's bedroom." She replaced the pillows and smoothed down the satin shams. "We'll fan out toward each other. Start at the ceiling of each room and work our way down to the floor. Be methodical. Tops of closets, backs of drawers, under beds and chairs, behind the books. It'll be a thick packet, right? You said about four hundred pages?"

"But maybe she divided it into chapters and scattered them around."

"Whatever. I'll know it when I see it, even if it's chopped up in parts, like a chicken." Marge stepped out of her loafers, pulled over a boudoir chair and climbed onto it to reach the top of a Georgian highboy. She felt around in the dust but found nothing. She brushed off her fingertips on her jeans.

"Go on," she said. "Shoo. Start in Henrietta's bedroom, then go to her dressing room. There must be a ton of hiding places in there."

Bridey hesitated, standing in the doorway that connected the two bedrooms, still reluctant to get started. That spooky feeling was shivering up the back of her neck; she knew she was asking for trouble.

"I don't know, Marge," she said uneasily. "This is going to take forever. There are the guest rooms, the maid's room, the laundry room. Eighteen rooms, for God's sake."

"Right. But there'll only be seventeen left to go when I finish in here, and only sixteen after you do Henrietta's bedroom, and you're not going to find it anywhere if you don't get moving." Even as she spoke, Marge climbed down from the chair and pushed it back into its place near the draperied window. She felt beneath the cushion and then ran a smoothing hand over it.

"I know," Bridey said, still standing in the doorway. "I know. I'm stalling. This is so scary!"

Marge turned to her, hands on her hips. "Now you just listen to me, Bridey Berrigan. Old Mrs. Willey wanted her book to be found. I just know it. I can feel it. I work with writers all the time. I know how they think. So stop spinning your wheels and start hunting."

"All right. All right! I'm going."

And Bridey went.

"But just so you know," she called back over her shoulder, "I don't feel good about this!"

Bridey explored every possible space, every drawer, every cushion, every fold of fabric in Henrietta's bedroom, from cornices down to the dust ruffle. She slid under the bed, reaching with an exploring hand to all four corners, and even looked out the window, as though the elusive manuscript might somehow be suspended out there, twelve floors above the sidewalk.

But there was nothing.

In the dressing room, she opened every hatbox, felt through every garment bag and shoe holder, ran her hands inside the stored fur coats and dug through the stacked-up containers of winter clothing.

Still nothing.

Meanwhile, Marge finished up in Neville's bedroom and moved on, first to his bathroom, where she combed through every shelf and drawer, even moving his matched hairbrushes, his old-fashioned straight razor and his jar of shaving soap, as though, small though they were, they might be hiding something, and then to his dressing room, where she pulled out shoe boxes and dug through piles of sweaters, shirts and ties.

Still there was nothing.

Silk and Satin ran back and forth between Bridey and Marge, as though urging them on, supervising their efforts, mewing excitedly, being pains in the neck.

An hour passed, and the two women were by then barefoot, disheveled and totally frustrated. Marge had broken a fingernail and Bridey had bruised her knuckles pulling a storage box off a shelf. They agreed they needed a break and went into the kitchen, where Bridey poured out a couple of Cokes and broke open a bag of chips. The cats prowled around their feet impatiently, rubbing their heads against the girls' ankles.

"This is making me nervous," Bridey said, plopping onto the chair at her desk. "It's like there are ghosts all around and we're digging in their graves. I can practically hear them wailing at us."

"I know," Marge said. "Isn't it exciting?" She was perched on the countertop, scattering potato-chip crumbs about as she waved her hands and wiggled her bare toes. "I feel like Nancy Drew. And I bet when that manuscript turns up, it's going to be right here in this kitchen. I can feel it, like when you play Hot and Cold. As soon as we came in here, I could hear those ghosts going 'Warmer, warmer . . .'"

"It can't be in here," Bridey said. "I work in this room all the time. I'd have come across it by now."

"Well, then, in the sewing room. That was Henrietta's sanctuary. That's where she hid her diary. I'll bet that's it."

"But no," Bridey said, "it should be in the library. That's where a manuscript belongs."

"Well, I can't stand this goofing off," Marge said, hopping down from the counter and brushing crumbs off her fingers. "Let's get back to the search. Onward and upward!"

"Okay, excelsior it is," Bridey said, forcing enthusiasm. "If I don't die of the stress first."

• • •

Two more hours passed, and the manuscript still hadn't turned up, not in the kitchen, not in the sewing room, not even in the library. Marge had already worked her way through the living room and the foyer and gotten well into dismantling the family room, and Bridey had reached the linen closet near the laundry room and was just replacing the towels on their shelves when she heard a shriek from her friend.

"Bridey! Come quick! Omigod, Bridey! Omigod! Come here!"

Bridey dropped everything and ran down the hall to the family room, where Marge was sitting on the floor, a big storage box between her legs and a mass of papers, mementoes and assorted oddments strewn about her randomly. Her face was wild and her hair was a mess. She was waving a pack of papers in the air, looking as though she'd discovered gold.

"This is it! I've got it! I found it! Oh, I don't believe it! I was right! It's here! Oh, Bridey, I was right!" Marge's cheeks were red with excitement. "She didn't burn it! It was right here, tucked away in a cabinet, behind this stack of old photos. Just waiting for us to come along and unearth it. Oh, I'm so excited! This is so totally awesome!"

An electric chill ran up Bridey's arms, and the hair at the back of her neck was crackling sharply. She dropped down on the floor next to Marge.

"Let me see it!" She grabbed the thick sheaf of papers out of Marge's hands.

It was true. There, on the cover page, was typed out:

## The Henrietta Lloyd Caswell Willey Book of Good Eating

Bridey was actually holding in her hands the very manuscript that had precipitated so much fuss. About 400 typewritten pages, a little crackly and yellow after all these years, but clearly Henrietta's cookbook/memoir. A faded pink ribbon was tied around the packet, and a note, hand-written in Henrietta Willey's characteristically flamboyant strokes, had been slipped under the small bow.

*There are none to follow me,* the note said. *This was my baby, the only one I ever had, and it died aborning.*

The papers trembled in Bridey's shaking hands.

"Oh, how awful! All that work, all that hope, all those dreams, all shot down by a single thoughtless rejection. The disappointment must have been unbearable. I feel so sorry for her."

Then Bridey stared thoughtfully at the title page. "Still, if it had been mine, I would never have given up on it so easily. I'd have fought for my work."

"I know," Marge said, grabbing the manuscript back from her. "But it doesn't surprise me all that much. I've known authors so devastated by a first rejection, they turned all their disappointment into a rage against their own work. Even pitched their manuscripts into the nearest fire."

"Well, thank God Henrietta didn't go that far." Bridey tugged at the manuscript, finally getting it back from Marge, who gave it up reluctantly. "But Marge, think what she did. Instead of fighting back, Henrietta turned all her humiliation and anger against Mr. Brewster and his family. What a stupid waste. As though Harmon and Brewster was the only publishing house in town. So foolish."

Bridey undid the ribbon, casting it aside impatiently. She leafed through several pages, skimming quickly, pausing occasionally here and there to read a paragraph closely. To her surprise, she found that the reminiscences were charming, the flamboyance of Henrietta's natural style carrying the sparkle of real life, the recipes reflecting genuine sophistication and culinary experience. Though the writing was obviously that of an amateur, there was interesting material in Henrietta's manuscript, material that deserved an audience.

She felt like shaking the old woman for giving up her baby so easily, for retreating into a stubborn rage, for preferring to nurse her unquenchable resentment instead of fighting back, trying again.

She looked up from the manuscript and into the living room, where no light at all remained, where

Henrietta's portrait had disappeared into the darkness.

Inevitably, she remembered Mack's oh-so-casual support of his father's judgment.

*I'd have done the same thing,* he'd said.

Would he really? she wondered. Would he really have been so abrupt, so thoughtless, so inconsiderate of an old woman's dream?

For hours Mack had been tramping up and down the streets of Manhattan. He didn't return to his apartment until almost ten o'clock, but by then he'd made some decisions.

He set all the lights in the living room blazing, stripped off his jacket and tossed it onto the sofa, loosened his tie and opened the top button of his shirt. He dropped into a deep armchair and, with his jaw set grimly, put the photo of his father onto the coffee table, where he could face it directly. He rolled up the sleeves of his shirt and leaned forward with his arms resting on his knees. The image in the picture peered back at him from its silver frame, and the two men, so alike in feature and expression, seemed squared off for serious battle. Mack breathed deeply a couple of times. Now he was ready to take on his father.

"Okay, Dad," he said firmly, "you and I are going to have a little talk."

He raked his hands through his hair, messing up the thick waves. This wasn't going to be easy.

"When you died, I figured we'd had our last fight. But now it looks like we're going to have to go one more round. You were always one tough old son of a bitch, Dad, and you never made room for anyone else's feelings or opinions. But maybe, where you are now, you're a little bit better able to hear me. So here's what I have to say.

"I always respected you. You know I did. And you know that I live by the rules you taught me. You taught me to value honor and loyalty. You taught me to be strong and sure of myself, to work hard, to take command. To be a leader of men. You taught me to treat our work, the work of book publishing, with respect and affection, to understand its great significance, but also to be tough and efficient in running the business. And to never forget the bottom line."

Here, Mack passed his hand across his mouth and jaw. He paused, needing a moment to choose his words.

"Okay. I know what you're going to say. You're going to say that those are good rules, and no one ever went wrong living by them. And I agree, Dad, up to a point. Like I said, I accepted your rules and I live by them. But I've discovered something else. I've discovered that strength can turn into cruelty.

"Now, I know you were never consciously or deliberately cruel. That would have been the grossest violation of the code you lived by. But take for example this matter of Henrietta Willey.

Remember, Dad? She gave you a manuscript to read many years ago, and you rejected it. That was okay, that was your call; Harmon doesn't publish cookbooks, no problem with that. But Dad, I've read over the correspondence in the file, and jeez, you really did drop the ball on that one. Your rejection letter was totally without consideration. The old lady had put a ton of love and work into that book, and she was your neighbor and you'd been a guest in her home. Okay, maybe she expected special attention, but that was the code she'd lived by. You knew that about her. Don't you think you could have given her feelings just a tad more consideration? Couldn't you have acknowl-edged all that effort instead of dismissing it out of hand? You knew perfectly well she expected at least a sympathetic reading. Would that have been so hard? Would it have cost you so much to have said a kind word?

"All right, so she was irascible and stubborn. But you were, too, you know. You and Henrietta were both too stubborn for your own good. And out of all that came this stupid feud between our families and this crazy obsession with the apartment next door. That's what it became, Dad, an obsession. As though I need another eighteen rooms for myself. It's absolutely ridiculous. I don't even have a family. Not yet . . ."

Mack paused again, his thoughts momentarily heading in a different direction.

241

"Though maybe, if—" he cut away from that thought before he got to it—"but we can talk about that later." He forced himself back to the matter at hand. "Anyway, this is to let you know that from here on, there will be some changes at Harmon and Brewster. I promise I won't scuttle the ship, but I'm going to run the firm with a lighter and a more considerate touch." Mack leaned back in the chair, satisfied he'd made his point. He smiled broadly.

"And you can trust me on that," he added.

And with those words, he felt the tension flow out of him and knew the first ease he'd had in days. The confrontation with his father had cleared out his demons, driven them all away, and left him with his peace of mind fully restored.

He got out of the chair, went into the kitchen, made a peanut butter sandwich, poured a big glass of milk and brought them back to the living room.

It was getting easier to win arguments with his father, now that the old man was dead. And now that the dust of battle had settled, he was ready to move on to the next item on his agenda.

Actually, Mack really liked discussing business matters with his father, who was, for him, still a partner and most trusted adviser; he now addressed his father's picture as though the two men were in conference on a matter relating directly to Harmon & Brewster's concerns.

"Now, about this other matter . . ."

He took a big bite of his sandwich and talked enthusiastically through the peanut butter.

"There's this girl, Dad, a really special girl—well, I'll be telling you more about her later." He gestured with his sandwich toward the photo and gulped down a swallow of milk to clear his palate. "But here's the thing. This girl is writing a book, too. Not our usual kind—I'm afraid it's in some ways very much like Mrs. Willey's, which you rejected—but I've been thinking. Maybe it's something Harmon and Brewster should consider. Now, before you object, let me explain that even though it is only a cookbook, it has a valuable slant: family history. Gives me an idea for a whole line—maybe a new imprint—let me just run it by you, Dad, before you object. These are personal stories, memoirs with a historical-social perspective, the big changes in women's lives. We would use these women's diaries, their recipe collections, the record of their domestic events—everyday stuff—and bring it into the twenty-first century, with good photos . . ."

He was enthusiastic now, spinning out new ideas.

On the floor of the family room in 12A, Bridey and Marge were still sitting cross-legged, paging together through Henrietta's manuscript, ignoring the mess that lay scattered all around them.

"You know, Bridey, this is really good stuff,"

Marge said thoughtfully. She had gotten her reading glasses from her bag, and with the skinny tortoiseshell rims perched on her nose, she was an incongruous mix of wild-haired hippie and high-powered executive as she carefully examined the couple of chapters she had wrested away from Bridey. "With the right editor . . ."

"Absolutely. I absolutely agree."

"No, I'm serious." She took off her glasses and looked intently at Bridey.

"So am I."

"No," Marge said. Her giddy excitement was gone now and she was all business. "No, what I mean is, *Lady Fair* really could use this. We'd have to buy the rights from the estate, of course— I'll get our legal guys on it first thing tomorrow— and we'd do a whole spread on this apartment, too. It's a natural."

"Whoa! You're going too fast."

"Not at all. Come on, let's clean up this junk." She waved her hand at the odds and ends that lay scattered about them, the stuff she'd pulled out of the cabinet along with the storage box, the family photos and old postcards and silly knickknacks, souvenirs of the Willeys' travels, childhood mementoes, stuff that had been packed together with the manuscript, stuff she'd tossed about in her excitement. "Let's just pack it all back where I found it and take this book off to a copy center."

Bridey started to gather various items from the

floor, while Marge was busy replacing the ribbon around the manuscript, tying a careless bow.

"I need a couple of rubber bands," Marge said, "just for safety." She glanced up briefly as though maybe a rubber band was lying there on the floor, just waiting to jump into her fingers. "Look around, see if you can find some. Maybe you could dig up a couple in the library."

But Bridey didn't respond.

"Bridey?"

Bridey still didn't answer, and Marge looked up from the manuscript in her hands.

Bridey was on her knees, staring at a small wooden box she was holding in her hands, a box about the size of a loaf pan. Her face had gone pale, and the spooked look was back in her eyes.

"What's this doing in here?" she said.

There was an unnatural quiver in her voice.

"What's what doing in here?" Marge went on tying.

"My Merrill box."

Marge glanced over casually and read the name on the little brass plate. She'd seen Bridey's recipe box a hundred times and couldn't see anything odd about it. Just the same old wooden box Bridey had treasured through all the years she'd known her. The same old box, scratched and worn, with the little brass plate on top and the name Merrill etched on it.

"I don't know. Where should it be?"

Even as she said it, it dawned on her that it

shouldn't be in the family room, mixed in with Henrietta's junk.

"It should be in the kitchen. That's where I always keep it. How did it get in here?" Bridey was so pale, her face was like milk.

"Beats me. Poltergeists?"

"Don't be funny, Marge. This is scary."

"Maybe one of the cleaning people moved it. Or something. You look terrible, Bridey. Are you all right?"

Bridey stood up shakily. Without a word, she walked out of the room, still holding the box in one hand.

In a moment she was back, and she was not only paler than ever, absolutely all the color had drained out of her face and tiny blue veins could be seen under her skin. She looked helplessly at Marge.

Silently, she held out two identical Merrill boxes, one in each hand.

# Chapter Nineteen

They both stared at the two boxes.

"Omigod," Marge whispered.

Bridey's hands were shaking and her mouth kept opening and then closing as her mind tried to make sense of what she was seeing. The impossible was taking shape in her head, but there were no words yet to give it expression.

"You'd better sit down," Marge said. "You look awfully pale."

Bridey sank to the floor.

"Let me get you some water." Marge ran into the nearest bathroom, grabbed a glass and filled it from the tap. When she got back, Bridey was still staring at the two boxes.

There was no question about it. They were identical, both of them scratched and worn, the brass hinges and clasps equally discolored with age. Each had its little brass plate on top, and the name Merrill was etched on both.

Unsteadily, Marge set the glass on the floor, ignoring the splashes that fell on the carpet. She took the two boxes from Bridey's unresisting fingers and put them down next to the glass.

"Here, drink this."

Bridey obediently drank a few sips. Then she raised her eyes to Marge's.

"What does it mean, Marge?" Her voice sounded ghostly.

Marge shook her head. She was turning pretty pale herself. "I don't know," she said.

They sat for a long time, just staring at the boxes.

Finally, as though she was afraid of her own voice, Marge whispered the words they were both thinking. "You're going to have to open it."

Bridey's head barely moved, nodding slightly in unwilling agreement. "I know."

Her eyes never left the boxes.

"Should I do it for you?" Marge asked.

Bridey took a huge, deep breath. She squared her shoulders. "No. I'll do it."

There was no question of her mixing up the two boxes; each of the little nicks and scratches on her own Merrill box was totally familiar to her. She reached out her shaking hand toward the other, flipped the catch with her thumbnail and lifted the lid, cautiously, as though she expected a trick snake to come flying out at her.

But no snake came flying out. It was just another box filled with cards, many of them frayed and stained from years of use, packed thickly together. Bridey knew, even before she got up the courage to inspect them, that they were recipe cards. What else could they be? And she already knew, with a chill running through her, that among them she would find duplicates of cards in her own box.

As though her fingers recognized them without her conscious help, she pulled out the oldest ones, the most yellowed and most frayed, and sure enough, there they were, like eerie messengers from another world: small, domestic treasures that belonged to a time long gone, to the time when Bridey's great-grandmother's grandmother first wrote them down.

There was Jane Merrill's recipe for a hundred-weight of souse—pickled pigs' feet and ears—

made with her special blend of spices. And her recipes for curd tarts and rabbit pie and whortleberry pie. For Indian cake and plum duff and blancmange, for "dough-nuts" flavored with rose water or lemon brandy with just a gill of lively emptings, "should you be lacking an egg."

"Emptings?" Marge asked, looking over Bridey's shoulder.

"Sort of like yeast," Bridey answered abstractedly, without looking around, still reading.

There were the recipes for carrot pie and hasty pudding and bird's nest pudding ("of a quantity of pleasant apples"), and there were directions for making soap and for cleaning white kid gloves by rubbing them with cream of tartar, and remedies for the sick, and arrowroot jelly made with loaf sugar and brandy.

They were all there, Jane Hamilton Merrill's secrets from the 1800s. But how could it be? It made no sense.

"Oh, Bridey." Marge's voice was almost a squeak. "This is giving me goose bumps. Look!" She held up her arm for Bridey to see.

Bridey didn't look up to see Marge's goose bumps. She had plenty of her own. Fearfully, but unable to stop herself, she felt at the back of the box where, sure enough, a piece of parchment had been placed. The words on the parchment were exactly what she'd known would be there.

To my dearest daughter on the occasion of her wedding, and to all the daughters who will come after—may you and yours always know the joy of skilled cookery, the comfort of wise economy and the fruit of honest industry.

Beneath that paragraph, the following had been added:

Henrietta, my dear. Your great-great-grandmother, Jane Hamilton Merrill, wrote that simple blessing long ago, and it has been passed down to the daughters of each generation ever since, along with these recipes. Now, on this happy day, it is your turn to receive them. May you and your darling Neville have many years of joy and good fortune.

Bridey gasped audibly as she read her own ancestor's name, her heart thumping violently. When she spoke, her voice sounded strangled, as though ordinary speech had become impossible.

"Look at this, Marge." She handed the parchment to her friend. "And now look at this." Out of her own Merrill box, she pulled a similar parchment, long since yellowed with age, and gave that one to Marge. The same words were written at the top.

> To my dearest daughter on the occasion of
> her wedding, and to all the daughters who
> will come after . . .

Marge read the two parchments, comparing them, her eyes going from one to the other several times.

"I don't get it," Marge said. "How can they be the same?"

"I don't get it either. Mine was given to my mother on the day she got married. And look," she pointed to the words below, "look at what her mother wrote at the bottom."

> My dear, dear Mary. This collection was
> begun by Jane Hamilton Merrill, your great-
> great-grandmother, and it is with much
> joy that I pass it on to you on this, your
> wedding day, and add my own blessing to
> hers. I pray that you and Kieran will know
> only good fortune in the years ahead.

"Kieran." Bridey whispered the names. "Mary and Kieran. My mother and father . . ."

"I feel like I'm in a time warp," Marge said. "Things like this don't happen."

"No. No, they don't."

They looked helplessly at all the papers strewn about, at the photos and the letters. And the *box*.

"This is so scary," Marge said.

"I know," Bridey whispered. "I know."

They both were silent for a very long time while the shock of what they were seeing began to sink in. Then, finally, Bridey's brain began to function. She looked around the room. She saw all the papers and photos tossed about on the floor.

"Maybe we should go through some of this stuff. Maybe we can find something to explain . . ."

Marge was already collecting papers.

"Here's some old wedding pictures," she said, gathering up a bunch. She brought them to Bridey. "Maybe they'll tell us something."

Carefully, so as not to damage the brittle paper that was already cracking in several places, Bridey examined an old wedding photo. In the center was the bride, a slim, delicately featured girl in an old-fashioned gown, the train fanned out, circling her feet. Her headdress was a simple band drawn back over bright, crinkly hair, with rosettes over each ear and the veil flowing back from her face. The groom, tall, dark and strikingly handsome in gray trousers and a cutaway coat, held her hands in his, and bridesmaids were ranged on either side of them. Bridey turned over the photo and read what was written on the back. *Caroline and Colum on their wedding day,* it said, *with Emily and the other bridesmaids.*

Bridey was staring blankly into space, as though the past had suddenly parted its veil and she could make out what was revealed there.

"Caroline was my grandmother's name," Bridey said, barely getting the words out. "She was married to Colum Connors. She died before I was born, and I never knew her maiden name. When my parents were killed in that car crash and I went to live with my father's family, they just called her Grandma Connors."

She was still sitting on the floor, feeling as though her bones had gone weak, and the cats nuzzled up to her, rubbing their faces against her legs. Silk patted the picture gently, and Bridey absentmindedly lifted it up, out of her reach.

Marge was staring at Bridey as though her friend had suddenly grown an extra head. She took the photo from Bridey and handed her a couple of papers folded in quarters. In a voice that seemed awestruck, she said, "What about these?"

As Bridey opened the papers, the folded edges ripped slightly. She handled them as carefully as she could and read aloud from the first, the writing spidery fine and faded.

Dearest Emily, There has been a fearful row and your father is so furious I can't persuade him even to speak to Caroline. He says she is dead to him forever. Colum is determined to return to Ireland, and Caroline must go with him, of course. Perhaps she will listen to her sister, though you are so much older. Do write to her, dear, and see if you can soften her heart. She and Colum say they will cut all ties to the family—oh, I cannot bear to write these words—and your father says that henceforth she will no longer be his child and he will never again speak her name. Oh, my dear, you cannot imagine how I suffer, for of course I must stand with your father in this—but how can people allow such foolish arguments to sever them from all they hold precious?

Your heartbroken Mother

She stared at the letter in her hands, rereading it silently several times, touched to the heart by its sad message. "I knew my grandmother came to this country sometime in the late sixties," Bridey said softly, "but I never realized . . . could that be why my father's family never spoke her maiden name?"

Marge shrugged in confusion. "If she was the same Caroline Connors . . ." She pointed to the other letter. "What does that one say?"

Bridey opened it and read:

Emily. It is with a heavy heart that I write these words. I have received your letter, and I respond in haste as we are all packed and are about to make our departure. Your words have cut me to the quick and I can think only that you, who are so much older than I, have forgotten what it is to love one man above all other things, even—dare I say it?—even one's own mother and father. But if I am dead to my family, then so it must be. We Lloyds are indeed a stubborn lot—stubbornness seems to run in our blood—and in this matter I, too, shall remain stubborn to the end. Farewell, Emily, and let this be the last communication between us. Your sister no more, Caroline Connors.

Bridey stared at the faded lines for a long time, lost in thought. Then suddenly the color flowed back into her face, and her eyes widened. She carefully refolded the letters, handed them to Marge and jumped up.

She ran out of the room. In the kitchen, where she'd left her tote bag, was the long family tree she'd been given at the kinship hearing. She dug about frantically for it, finally finding it stuffed in among subway maps, a receipt for three pairs of socks from The Gap and a half-finished crossword puzzle clipped from the *New York Times*. She ran back to the family room, where Marge was still gazing dumbstruck at nothing at all. She spread out the family tree on the floor, all seven feet of it, and got down on all fours to examine it. With one finger, she traced the line back from

Henrietta through Emily Lloyd to Henrietta's grandmother, Catherine Morton, who was married to Henry Lloyd. Catherine and Henry had had two daughters, but Mulie had been interested only in their eldest, Emily—Henrietta's mother.

"But look," Bridey said, pointing to the next box in the row. "I *knew* I'd seen that name. Here it is." Her finger rested on the paper. "Emily had a younger sister. And her name was Caroline!"

"But that could mean . . ." Marge came to a dead stop. For once in her life, she was having trouble finding the words.

"Yes," Bridey continued. "If the two Carolines were actually the same person," she felt a shudder run up her spine as she spoke the impossible words aloud, "then Emily's sister and my Grandma Connors were the same person."

Marge was silent. She was staring at her friend as though Bridey had sprouted wings.

"And look, Marge." Bridey's finger went back along the family tree. "Look at the dates when Caroline's parents died. Henry in 1958 and Catherine in 1963. My Grandma Connors—if she was their daughter—didn't leave Ireland until after Catherine had died. Maybe she was unwilling to return until after her parents were gone."

"Oh, Bridey," Marge said. "I practically don't dare say it." She took a breath and then continued. "That would mean, you and Henrietta—"

"Don't even say it, Marge. I mean, they're

common enough names—how could it—I mean, it couldn't possibly be, but—" She had to stop because she couldn't bring herself to say the words.

Marge said them for her. "That would make you—"

"I don't know what it would make me. But if it were true, it would make me and Henrietta some kind of . . . something. I don't know what."

"Well, some kind of cousins, I think."

"Omigod."

"You said it. Omigod is right. What are you going to do?"

Bridey sat silently for a long minute. Then she sat back on her heels.

"I know what I'm going to do. I'm going to call Mr. Kinski. I'll let him tell me what it means."

"And if it means what I think it means—"

"Don't say it, Marge. Don't even think it! Just hand me the phone."

Marge listened breathlessly while Bridey dialed. Together, they waited through several rings before there was an answer.

"I know it's late," she heard Bridey say, obviously in response to a sleepy Gerald Kinski. "But I have to talk to you now. Either that or spend a sleepless night."

Marge settled into a big comfy armchair while Bridey told the attorney everything: how they'd decided to hunt for the manuscript, how they'd discovered Henrietta's duplicate Merrill box, the letters and photos, the coincidences of names and dates, the whole crazy, improbable, impossible story.

Then she heard Bridey say, "Now? But it's almost midnight, and I thought—" Then there was a long pause while Bridey listened to what was being said on the other end. "Well, I know, Mr. Kinski," she said at last. "Seventy million dollars do kind of make an exception, and if you're sure you don't mind . . ." There was another pause, and then Bridey said, "That's fine, Mr. Kinski. In half an hour." She hung up, and her face was shining with excitement.

"What's up?" Marge asked.

"He wants us to get all this stuff together and bring it down to his office right away. He says he wants to look at it carefully, and if it looks authentic, he can put his staff on it first thing in the morning to get it all documented. He says it shouldn't be too difficult to find the necessary records: certificates of birth, marriage, that kind of thing. Oh, Marge, look! My hands are shaking." She put her hand on her chest. "My heart's going so fast, I think it's going to pop."

"Not yet, sweetie. We've got to get cracking." Marge was already on her hands and knees, making neat piles of all the papers and photos, packing them into the file box. "Can I go, too?"

"Are you kidding? Don't leave me for a minute! Someone's got to hold my hand."

In twenty minutes they'd gathered all the evidence, sealed up the box, straightened things up and were ready to leave.

Bridey wasn't ready for any more surprises on this most extraordinary evening, but just as she opened the door, there was Mack, his hand upraised, about to knock.

"Bridey?" he said, astonished to see her. His hand dropped slowly. "I know it's late, but I couldn't sleep, and I saw the light on in your kitchen so I knew you were still up. I have to talk to you—" His eyes went to the big storage box she was just lugging up from the floor. Then he saw Marge. "But I didn't realize—"

He did indeed look sleepless, with a kind of intensity burning in his eyes and a rumpled air that was quite uncharacteristic of him, as though he'd just passed through a whirlwind. His hair was uncombed, he needed a shave and he seemed to have just tossed on the handiest clothes: jeans, a casual shirt, no socks, just a pair of worn Top-Siders. But to Bridey, who was in a whirlwind of her own, the arrival of Mack at her door at that very moment served to ease her disheveled state of mind. To her surprise, while she could remember thinking she'd never talk to him again, all her anger suddenly evaporated, and she felt as though a platform, rock solid and steady, had just been slipped beneath her feet. She looked into those dark eyes and found she was eager to tell him about their uncanny discovery. No, more than eager; she needed to tell him.

"This is my friend, Marge Webster," she said, nodding her head in Marge's direction. Having taken in the situation, her friend had closed the door behind her and slithered past Mack and Bridey to ring for the elevator.

"And you," Marge smiled wickedly, "must be Mack, the cute guy next door." She was eyeing him up and down, taking in the handsome face, the good body, the casual appearance, the bit of beard stubble. "I've been hearing about you."

She grinned at Bridey, who glared back at her furiously and colored violently, right to the roots of her bright hair.

Mack also colored.

"I can imagine. Here," he said, turning to Bridey and taking the awkward box out of her hands. "Let me help you with that. I'll put it on the elevator for you." He paused, searching for the right words. Marge's presence had thrown him off stride, but there was so much he needed to say, he decided to go for it. "Will you be gone long? If I don't get to talk to you tonight, I'm not going to be able to sleep."

"Why don't you come along?" Bridey said. She was eager to have him with her. "I could use a support group tonight."

Mack's eyebrows rose. "What's happening?" he asked, just as the elevator arrived. "I hadn't expected to find you going out at this hour."

"Just wait till you hear," she said as she nodded to Sandor. "I'll tell you about it in the cab."

# Chapter Twenty

Ten minutes later, it was a stunned Mack who needed to be told that the cab had arrived at its destination. He'd forgotten why he'd been driven, helplessly, to knock on Bridey's door. Now he was staring incredulously at her. Coming on top of the emotional turmoil he'd just put himself through, her hurried account of the evening's discoveries had put him into stimulus overload; he felt as though his head and heart had been pried open and filled with a buzzing, dazzling confusion, all sweet, strange and incredibly mysterious. Her story made no sense to him, for it was all too unbelievable. And yet how could he not believe her? Her honesty was so utterly apparent, an inherent element of the irresistible spell she had cast over him. Mechanically, still staring blankly after her as she and Marge got out onto the sidewalk, he paid the driver, dragged out the big file box and followed the two women into the silent lobby of the darkened building.

Only one security guard was on night duty, and

he'd already been alerted by Gerald Kinski, who had only just arrived himself, to send Bridey up. Not a word was spoken as the three ascended in the elevator to the forty-third floor, where the lawyer was waiting for them.

It was obvious that Gerry, dragged from his bed, had dressed quickly. He wore only a white business shirt, open at the collar, a pair of gray slacks and tasseled loafers. He must have barely passed a comb through the thin remnants of his hair, for it was flying about in gray wisps, and his chin was stubbly. But his eyes were completely alert. Bridey's call had electrified him, and he was eager to see what she'd brought him. He barely acknowledged the presence of Marge and Mack as introductions were made.

"Nothing personal," he said as Mack set the box onto his desk, "but I want to be alone with Bridey. Would you two mind waiting in the reception area? I'd like to talk with my client privately."

*His client? Since when,* Bridey wondered, *did I become his client?* Things sure were happening fast.

"Oh, of course. Of course." Marge and Mack turned to leave the room.

"The overnight staff should have some coffee going," Gerald said, waving vaguely down the empty hall. "Just look in at the media station, last door on your left. They'll fix you up. I'll come and get you when we're ready." He was itching to get at those papers, and he could hardly wait for the door to close behind Marge and Mack.

"Now, Bridey," he said, turning toward her. He paused, took a deep breath and gave her a long, searching look. "This is a most extraordinary development. Unbelievable, in fact. Sit down, my dear. Sit down. Right there." He indicated the client chair. "Just make yourself comfortable and tell me all about it. Leave out nothing."

Bridey perched nervously on the edge of the chair. The story seemed even crazier now that she had to recount it. But there was nothing to do but tell him every detail, beginning with the history of Henrietta Willey's manuscript, how they had hunted for and found it, and the discovery of the duplicate Merrill box, the photos and the letters, and their apparent connection to her.

Gerald's mouth was hanging open by the time she finished.

He said nothing for a long time. Then, abruptly, as though remembering his manners, he closed his mouth, but still he seemed unable to make any comment.

When at last he did speak, he could say only one word. "Well!"

And then he repeated it, several times. "Well, well, well."

He was eyeing her carefully, for he had learned to be cynical about clients' machinations, and $70 million could make pretty tempting bait. He would have to determine whether her story was genuine, but no matter how piercingly he searched her expression, he saw nothing in the openness of her face but her own authentic confusion, even dismay.

And anyway, with the information she'd produced out of that file box, it would be a simple job to have the staff run down all the supporting documents: routine checks at the Bureau of Vital Statistics and in the appropriate church and county records. Those papers she'd brought in would tell them where to look.

"This changes everything," he said. "If it all checks out, we'll move immediately for a second kinship hearing based on newly discovered information. We'll have to act fast . . ."

But the whole thing was too incredible. Just too amazingly incredible. Just wait till Doug and Art heard about this. What a way to regain all those lost points!

Visions of trustees' fees on a $70-million estate, fees he'd thought were gone forever, swam seductively back into view.

Waiting tensely in the empty reception area, Mack and Marge were into a very interesting conversation of their own. Steaming black coffee had given them a caffeine boost, and Marge's thoughts had been busy in all directions, including a quick note to herself: *I can see why Bridey fainted. The man's a doll!*

But his first words jolted her into a whole other direction.

"I've been thinking," Mack was saying. "I'd like to review that manuscript of Henrietta's. Our publishing house might have an interest in doing something with it. . . ."

"Oh no you don't!"

No matter how long and exhausting a night it had been, when it came to acquiring a good property for *Lady Fair*, Marge was instantly and totally awake, any time of the day or night.

"No you don't," she repeated. "You had your shot at it. Now it's my turn."

"Now wait a minute," Mack said sharply. He set his Styrofoam cup onto the table in front of him. He hadn't expected any opposition; quite the contrary, he'd thought she'd like the idea. "In our hands, that manuscript can get the play it deserves. With our marketing and distribution capabilities, with the name of Harmon and Brewster behind it—"

"Are you kidding? Can Harmon and Brewster match a national circulation of four point seven million? You can't even contemplate a first print run of anything like that. Not for a cookbook. Your house has no experience with that kind of material, but it's just our readers' thing. It's a natural for us, and—"

"We'd be prepared to offer a substantial sum to acquire the rights—"

"Nothing like what *Lady Fair* would pay." Marge had forgotten all about Mack's cuteness quotient. She was all business now. "I have in mind a big photo spread as well: that fabulous apartment, Henrietta's elegant lifestyle, Neville's foreign diplomatic postings. It's a natural for us," she repeated. "Our readers would eat it up."

"We may be able to offer a package. We might consider adding Bridey's book, as well, to the mix."

"But that's just what I have in mind, too: a whole series of similar pieces—"

"Maybe with a deal for her next book as well—"

That one stopped Marge, but only briefly. She grasped at her first thought, hoping to bring his locomotive to a stop.

"But I can offer something you can't," she said. "Bridey and I have been best friends for years. If she signs with us, she'll be dealing with someone who genuinely has her welfare at heart, someone who loves her."

That one must have worked, because Mack went very quiet, and an odd expression passed over his face.

He wasn't about to say what was on his mind. Not to anyone but Bridey. But he was saved from having to counter Marge's argument by the arrival in the reception area of Bridey and Gerald Kinski.

Bridey looked wiped out. Now that everything had been turned over to Gerry, the emotional roller coaster of the last few hours had finally dumped her out, exhausted and confused. Her eyes looked weary and she seemed ready to fall over, as though her bones had lost all their strength.

But Marge was all live-wire energy, and she was unable to think of anything except her own ever-expanding plans.

"Bridey, sweetie! I've got some great ideas. Now just listen to this!"

Bridey stared blankly at her friend.

"What I've been thinking," Marge bubbled on, completely oblivious to her friend's empty gaze, "what you need—"

Mack interrupted her, bringing her up short. "Never mind about that now, Bridey," he said, shooting a warning glance at Marge. He was genuinely concerned and put a protective arm around her. "You look exhausted," he said as he led her toward the door. "I'm taking you home. The only thing you need now is a good night's sleep."

"That's a good idea," Gerry said. "You just get some rest. I'll handle everything from here on. And I'll be in touch in a day or two."

"Oh, of course, Bridey," Marge chimed in, following Bridey and Mack to the elevator. "Of course. I'm so sorry. I just got carried away. It can wait. You must be knocked out, sweetie. Get to bed now, and I'll give you a call tomorrow. We can talk then."

Downstairs, on the sidewalk, as Marge stepped into a cab, she said quietly to Mack, "Can we agree not to talk to Bridey about . . . well, about what we were talking about—publishing her work—"

She didn't need to finish. "Of course," Mack said. "She's much too tired to think about that now." He closed her door and they gave each other a friendly wave as Marge's cab pulled away.

And he was as good as his word. He and Bridey were silent all the way home. It wasn't till they were on the twelfth floor and she was letting herself into 12A that she turned to him to say good night.

"By the way," she said sleepily, "you were coming to see me earlier tonight. What was it you wanted to tell me?"

He looked deeply into her eyes, saw the fatigue there and decided to wait.

"Never mind," he said softly. "It'll keep."

# Chapter Twenty-one

When Marge called next morning, Bridey wasn't yet ready to wake up. "Later, Marge," she mumbled sleepily from the depths of her pillows. "Later." Her head never came out from under the covers and she fumbled the phone back onto the night table, even while Marge was still talking.

When Gerald Kinski called at noon, she was still too tired to talk.

"Can it wait till tomorrow?" she asked. "I'm just so bushed."

"Oh, sure, Bridey. Sure thing. I just wanted to let you know my people are working like a bunch of busy little beavers. But sure, no problem. It can wait till tomorrow. You just rest." And he hung up, too.

Two hours later, as the sun passed to the west, it sent its light across the terrace and through the bedroom window. The bright shaft touched Bridey's face, she turned her face away from the glare and a sleep-fogged question drifted through her sleepy head.

*Did I forget to draw the drapes?*

Usually, she was careful to keep those drapes closed, but last night's exhaustion had dropped her into bed without a thought for Mack's view into her bedroom from his terrace, or of anything else. But now, in her half-awake state, the memory of Mack floated through her head and, as though she was still dreaming, she contemplated the image that moved across the screen of her closed eyelids. Gradually, a series of questions formed: *What had he wanted last night, coming to the door so late? And he's such a model of spit-and-polish; why was he so disheveled? What was the silent message that had put such a fire in his eyes?*

She'd been too distracted to pay sufficient

attention to the change in him, but now, as the evening unscrolled in her memory, she realized how different he'd seemed. Now, in her mental photograph of him, he had softened and there was a new expression in his eyes, an expression she couldn't identify. What happened to all that starch?

*Is he out there now, on his terrace?*

In her half-sleep, with her eyes still closed, she let herself imagine him, tall and dark, at rest in one of the lounge chairs, perhaps taking care of work he'd brought home from the office with him, a stack of manuscripts on the wrought-iron table, a cup of coffee at hand, his nose buried in his notes, with Scout lazing at his side. Or perhaps he'd be writing one of those awful rejection letters, his laptop sitting on the table in front of him. Or, as one fantasy blended into the next, he was standing at the wall, looking lean and very manly, his arms resting casually on the rail-topped parapet, looking down on Park Avenue. Or perhaps he was looking up into the blue summer sky to catch the rare sight of a peregrine falcon, returning to its Chrysler Building aerie. Perhaps he turns and looks toward her, sees her there in her bed; he comes toward her, stepping over the low wall that separates his terrace from hers . . .

She'd been too tired last night to do more than peel off her clothes and drop them on the floor. She wore no nightgown. Now she murmured lazily to herself, feeling deliciously self-conscious, tucked under the covers with her fantasies. To reassure herself that she was covered, she ran her fingertips along the sheet's silken edge where it brushed her cheek.

The phone rang. With her eyes still closed, she reached for it and pulled it in under the covers.

"Are you feeling better?"

Startled, her eyes popped wide open and she sat up suddenly, grabbing at the sheet, as though he could see her. Involuntarily, she glanced toward the terrace. There was no one there.

"It's after two," Mack said. "Did I wake you?"

"Sort of," she stammered. His voice shocked her back to reality, the extraordinary events of the previous night swimming into focus. "I feel like I've been hit with a sledgehammer," she said. Could it all have been a dream? Or could the impossible have become real?

"Can we talk?"

Talk? Yes, she wanted very much to talk. She needed to reach out, to get a grip on reality. She remembered Gerry's call. Little beavers? It must be true. His busy little beavers were working on all those incredible documents. In the clear light of day, she had to recognize that no, she had not dreamed everything.

"I'm willing, as long as we don't talk about me and Henrietta. That's one subject I refuse to think about till I hear from Mr. Kinski tomorrow."

"No problem. I promise the name of that woman

will not pass my lips. Could we maybe just take a walk in the park? It's a beautiful day, the sun is shining, the birds are singing." He dropped his voice a little, coaxing her. "I'll buy you a hot dog."

She didn't need any coaxing. She looked toward the terrace again, then relaxed her grip on the sheet.

"With sauerkraut?"

"With anything you want."

She smiled, pleased.

"I'd really like that," she said.

She hung up the phone. The cats jumped onto the bed, and she stroked them thoughtfully.

"Well, something's happened to him. I thought he was such a stuffed shirt. Could I have been wrong?" She scratched at the soft fur along Silk's cheek. "What do you think, little mother?" The cat closed her eyes and stretched her neck luxuriously. "Could it be that I've been too stubborn?" Silk patted Bridey's arm encouragingly. "Do you think Mack Brewster has changed? Or could it possibly be that I'm the one who has changed?"

Gerald Kinski's associates were research experts. They knew exactly what they were looking for and it was a simple matter, using the resources of the Census Bureau, the Bureau of Vital Statistics, and the National Archives, to gather all the information they needed. Within hours the relevant documents had been faxed to the offices of Braye,

Kohler and Kinski, and by late afternoon a complete file was ready on Gerald's desk, with covering memorandums and all the pleadings necessary to move the court for a second kinship hearing. His busy beavers had done a good job, and as he read through the file, Gerry exulted excitedly. As improbable as it all was, everything checked out perfectly, everything fitted together like spoons in a drawer, like baby and mama, like the clues in a perfectly plotted mystery story.

"Oh, happy day!" he exclaimed to no one in particular. "If anyone had told me that something like this could happen . . ." He leafed through the papers one more time, reassuring himself that every *t* had been crossed and every *i* dotted, that every single item of proof was exactly in place and properly substantiated.

"This story is so unbelievable," he announced to an imaginary listener. "You can't make this stuff up!"

He paced his office once around to calm himself down. Then he hit the intercom button on his phone.

"Cynthia," he said, "I want you to schedule a meeting as soon as possible with Doug and Art. As soon as possible," he repeated, making sure she understood the urgency. "This is important."

Then he did a happy little jig in the middle of the room and pumped his fist. "Yes!"

He took a deep breath and dropped back into

his chair. "Afton Morley," he whispered triumphantly, "eat your heart out!"

Marge, in the meantime, was putting together all her ideas for the feature she planned. She'd slept only a few hours after leaving Bridey the night before, and she was at her desk early, dictating memos, sketching layouts and organizing her thoughts. By late afternoon, she'd already consulted with the legal department, the photo people and the food experts on her staff.

And while one corner of her mind was busy with all her planning, another had finally realized there was no reason to fight with Mack about acquiring the rights to Henrietta's manuscript. A tie-in with a book publisher could work to the advantage of *Lady Fair*. She decided to approach him about the possibilities of a cooperative effort, but by the time she called his office he'd already left for the day.

"Oh, nuts!" she said as she hung up the phone. When Marge was stalking a hot new idea, any impediment made her ferociously impatient. "Wouldn't you know. Just when I need to talk to him. He should be in his office. Why isn't he in his office?"

She strode to the window, glared down at the sidewalk, circled the room a couple of times, went back to the window and smacked her hand against the glass.

"Mackenzie Brewster, where are you?"

• • •

Mackenzie Brewster was right where he wanted to be.

He was in Central Park, strolling with Bridey along the edge of the Lake, where a couple of swans were swimming in graceful, lazy circles.

"Aren't they wonderful?" Bridey said.

"Wonderful," Mack said, not looking at them at all. His eyes were fixed on Bridey. It seemed to him that all beauty paled beside her. The sun was full on her lovely hair, a good night's rest had restored her color and he was entranced by a tiny smudge of mustard that decorated the corner of her mouth.

"Good hot dog?" he said.

"Perfect," she answered. "Just what I needed."

They continued silently for a while, following the path around the Lake and then turning to cross over the lovely Bow Bridge.

"Let's stop here," Mack said as they reached the top of the bridge. She was willing, and they went to the edge and rested their arms on the iron railing. Together, they gazed thoughtfully at the calm water below.

"You're awfully quiet," Bridey said.

"So are you."

"I'm trying not to think."

"Mmmm," he murmured. It must be hard, he thought, to avoid thinking about the fabulous fortune that was dangling promisingly in front of her. "You've got a lot to not think about," he said sympathetically.

"You promised we wouldn't talk about that," she cautioned.

"Right. We won't."

He was mindful of his promise and closed the door to that topic of conversation. He remembered another promise, too: the one he'd made to Marge not to talk to Bridey about his wanting to publish her cookbook.

That left only one subject.

"Let's talk about you and me," he said gently.

She didn't turn to look at him, but instead continued to stare into the water. He saw the color rise in her cheeks.

"That's not a forbidden subject, is it, Bridey?"

She still didn't turn, only shook her head slightly from side to side. Now her cheeks were bright pink.

Encouraged, he leaned a little closer to her.

"I've been such a horse's ass. No—" he waved off the polite objection she was about to make— "no, it's true; I have been. But last night I had a long talk with my dad. In fact, I told him off. And if you knew my dad, you'd know that's like talking down an angry lion. But thanks to you, I was able to set him straight about a couple of things, and I think I set myself straight, too."

"Funny, I'd been noticing a little unwarranted stubbornness on my part, too," Bridey said, glancing mischievously, sideways, at him. "And tell me, did your dad answer you back from the other side?"

"Nah." Mack's tone turned flippant, too. "He knew I was right. Anyway, I had more important things to tell him."

She raised her eyebrows quizzically.

"I told him about you," Mack said softly. "I told him I'd met a girl: a special girl, a girl who's turned me completely around—the girl of my dreams."

Bridey's breath caught in her throat and her heart thumped hard against her ribs. Once again, the color drained from her cheeks.

"A girl whose freckles show in the sunlight and who blushes sweetly when she's embarrassed."

He reached out a hand and touched her hair. "And whose hair is like moonlight and music."

"Oh, Mack . . ." She looked away, too overcome to face him.

"A girl who faints when I kiss her." He turned her toward him, reaching his arms around her. "And who's got a bit of mustard, just the tiniest bit, in the corner of her mouth right here. . . ."

And he kissed her. Long and tenderly. And then again, longer still, and more and more warmly, and the trees circled slowly over her head, and the bridge beneath her rocked back and forth, and he had to hold her firmly so she wouldn't faint again.

And she forgot that she'd ever been angry with him, for he was indeed the most wonderful man in the whole world, and fame and fortune were unimportant while he held her in his arms.

# Epilogue

Bridey's wedding dress was a replica of the one worn by her Grandmother Caroline. They had copied it from the faded, cracked photo they'd found among Henrietta's papers. Flowers were woven through her hair, and a soft veil fell gracefully from the band that circled her head. Her bouquet was an armful of calla lilies, tied with a broad ribbon of white satin, and as she walked down the aisle, an aura of grace and loveliness surrounded her.

For the rest of his life, Mack would remember—and always with a catch in his throat—how beautiful she looked that day.

Gerald Kinski gave her away, and he was as proud as any father as he walked her down the aisle.

Marge, whose wedding gift was a gorgeous crystal bowl from Lobmeyr, was striking in a simple suit of pale green linen, with only a small cluster of pearls in her dark hair.

Doug Braye and Art Kohler were there, too, looking as satisfied as a couple of well-fed tigers. Their gift, an exquisite sterling-silver coffee service from Tiffany, cost the firm a fortune, but nothing was too good for their best client, and anyway, their books would show it as a business expense, to be taken as a tax deduction.

Bridey's Grandma Berrigan was there, beaming proudly at the beautiful bride, and all the cousins and aunts and uncles were there, too. They were still a little awestruck at the incredible—the miraculous—good fortune that had come into her life, what with her sudden and practically inconceivable great wealth, the publication of her book and the appearance of her picture in *Lady Fair*. Grandma Berrigan carried the magazine everywhere with her, in case she ran into someone who, by some chance, hadn't seen it.

Present also was Gilbert Forsgren, the referee who had presided over the hearing at which it was determined that Bridey was indeed Henrietta's first cousin once removed, which was, of course, better than a first cousin twice removed. With him, also, was His Honor Vincent Mallory, the judge who had ruled, in a separate proceeding, that a natural heir had been found and, under the terms of Henrietta's will, the entire estate should therefore pass to Bridey, free of all claims and impediments. Of course, their invitations had not been sent until after they'd made their rulings, so as to avoid any hint of impropriety or any suggestion of an effort to influence their decisions.

The two men arrived together, bearing a joint wedding gift, the most recent edition of Greenwood's *The Researcher's Guide to American Genealogy*, updated to include the latest computer techniques.

But the special guests of honor were Silk and Satin, who rested on a white pillow on the front pew of the church, wearing festive white silk bows around their necks. Silk's babies, born only three weeks earlier, were of course too young to attend and remained at home, where they slept through the whole ceremony in their nest, which Bridey had fashioned out of the "magical" storage box that had contained the Merrill box, Henrietta's manuscript, the photos and all the documents that had revealed the connection between her and Henrietta Willey.

The wedding reception was held in the huge living room of apartment 12A, following the church ceremony. Bridey had planned the menu, from canapés to after-dinner mints, and, though she'd entrusted the food preparation to caterers, she'd insisted on making the wedding cake herself. She even agreed to allow Marge's best photographers to move discreetly among the guests, capturing wonderful pictures of the food, the clothes, the setting, even Silk and Satin and the kittens, to be published in *Lady Fair*'s next issue, along with recipes and text by Bridey herself.

Amid the music, the marvelous food and the general merrymaking, it was soon the kittens' turn to be the center of admiring attention, as one guest after another came into the cats' room off the kitchen to ooh and aah over the antics of the darling babies, each one an intriguing mix of blue-gray and midnight black. Silk stayed close to them, being careful that everyone kept a safe distance, while Satin retired to his own bed, waiting for all the racket to be done with.

Only Mrs. Maudsley, sipping coolly at her martini, found something to complain about.

"And now," she whispered to her husband, lifting her chin toward a beaming Mack, who had his arm around a glowing Bridey, "I suppose they'll be having a mob of kids, and the whole twelfth floor will be a gaggle of noisy children and animals." She sipped again at her martini. "What would the old girl have thought of that?"

"Oh, I don't know," Harold said. He glanced up at the portrait. "I get the feeling she'd be okay with it."

Indeed Henrietta was smiling down from her portrait as though it pleased her, now that everything had come out right, to see that once again her home was the scene of the perfect party. The guests were enjoying themselves, the food was perfect and the champagne flowed lavishly. And when Max the doorman and Tom the elevator operator dropped by to offer their best wishes on the merger of 12A and 12B, each of them was given a piece of cake and a glass of champagne.

Yes indeed. The old girl seemed to be happy about the whole thing.

# Bridey's Stews from Around the World

*Szekely Goulash* (from Hungary)

Maria Molnar and her husband, Gabor, run a little restaurant in Bridey's hometown, on Wren's Road in Warrentown, just off Route 9. Bridey had summer jobs in the restaurant while she was in high school, and it was in Maria's kitchen that Bridey discovered Hungarian cuisine, a wondrous mixture of Magyar, Turkish, Transylvanian and—from the days of Empire—Austrian.

1½ tablespoons oil or 2 tablespoons butter
1 large onion, diced
2½ tablespoons paprika
2 tablespoons tomato puree
½ teaspoon caraway seeds
1 bay leaf
2 pounds lean pork, cut in small cubes
1 bottle (12 oz.) light beer
2 pounds sauerkraut, very well drained
Salt to taste
¾ cup sour cream

In a large, deep pan or Dutch oven:

- Heat the oil (or butter), then add the diced onion and simmer gently till soft and golden.
- Sprinkle the paprika generously over the onion, stir all together and continue simmering for a couple of minutes.
- Stir the tomato puree and the caraway seeds well through the onion and simmer for another minute.
- Add the bay leaf.
- Add the pork, mix well with the onion and tomato mixture, add the beer and, if needed, enough water to cover all.
- Cover and simmer gently till the pork is almost done, 45 minutes to 1 hour.
- Squeeze the sauerkraut very dry, stir it well into the mixture, cover all and continue to simmer gently, 15 minutes or until the pork is done.
- Taste, add salt if needed and stir.
- Add the sour cream on top, cover, turn off the heat and let all sit for a few minutes till the sour cream is warm. (Or, if you prefer, turn the mixture onto a serving platter and then top it with the cold sour cream.)

Serve with flat noodles or dumplings.

### *Doro Wat* (Ethiopian Chicken)

When Bridey was in sixth grade, she did a geography report on Ethiopia. Her best friend's big sister, Beany Norquist, from across the street, was in the Peace Corps in East Africa, and she sent back this recipe to Bridey, along with a packet of berbere spices, the recipe for injera and instructions on how to use it to scoop up the stew—but only with her right hand!

¼ pound butter
½ cup water
3 large onions, diced
¾ cup water or light beer
6-ounce can tomato paste
1 whole chicken, cut into about 12 pieces
Hard-boiled eggs, peeled (1 for each person)
3 rounded tablespoons berbere (see note below)
1 teaspoon salt

In a large, deep pan or Dutch oven:

- Heat the butter, then add the diced onion and simmer gently till soft and golden.
- Stir the berbere into the onions together with ½ cup of water and simmer gently for about 5 minutes.

- Stir tomato paste into the onions together with another ¾ cup of water (or light beer), and simmer for another 30 minutes. (Stir frequently to avoid burning the pot.)
- Add the cut-up chicken, cover and let all cook together over very low fire for about 1 hour or until the chicken is soft. Stir frequently.
- During the last 10 minutes of the cooking, add the hard-boiled eggs. Make shallow slits in the egg whites to allow the juice to seep in.

The sauce should be rather thick; if it is too thin, allow some of the water to cook off.

And mop up the sauce with Ethiopia's crêpelike bread, injera. (See next recipe.)

Note: The berbere is a mixture of chili, coriander, cloves, cardamom, ajowan, allspice, black pepper, nigella, fenugreek seed, cinnamon and ginger.

Berbere spices used in Ethiopian cooking, such as ajowan and nigella seeds, are available online from Amazon and from Zamouri Spices, Kalustyan's Spices and Sweets and Nirmala's Kitchen.

*Injera* (Ethiopian crêpes)

3 cups all-purpose flour
1 cup buckwheat flour
2 tablespoons baking soda
1 teaspoon salt
4 cups club soda or light beer
1 cup rice vinegar
Oil for the pan

- To make the batter: In a large mixing bowl, stir together the two flours, baking soda, and salt. Slowly add the club soda or beer and stir until smooth. Add vinegar and stir.
- Heat a large skillet over medium heat. With a paper towel, wipe the skillet with cooking oil.
- Pour batter into the pan in a small circle.
- Swirl the batter around till it makes a thin pancake (up to 9 inches).
- After one minute, use a large spatula to flip the injera over and cook one more minute.
- Remove from the pan and stack up on a plate. The pancakes will soften as they cool.
- Serve with the Doro wat. Tear the injera in pieces and use the pieces to pick up the Doro wat.

*Chili con Carne* (Grandma Berrigan's version, feeds many)

Every year, at Halloween, the fall evenings were nippy in Warrentown, and the trick-or-treaters had to wear coats and mittens over their costumes. Grandma Berrigan would make up a big pot of chili and the kids would stop by on Bridey's front porch so her grandmother could warm them up with a bowl of hot chili handed out through the kitchen window. Her recipe required a lot of work, so she made it only once a year, but it was so good and so festive and so easy to spoon up, even with mittens on, it was well worth it.

Bridey likes to cook from scratch. But she's learned that some dishes are improved by a mix of fresh and canned ingredients. Her version of Grandma Berrigan's chili, for example, combines dry beans and canned, and also adds some canned chili to the pot.

Her recipe is very flexible and can be easily modified to suit any taste. Purists shouldn't object to the bottled ketchup. It works extremely well.

1½ pounds dry beans, any variety (1½ pounds, altogether)
cold water to cover, plus 2 inches
1 pound ground beef

1 pound sausage (hot or mild, to your taste; Bridey likes sweet Italian)

1 pound beef (round or chuck), cut in small chunks, as for stroganoff

1½ tablespoons olive oil

3 medium onions, diced

2 cloves minced garlic

¼ teaspoon black pepper

½ teaspoon marjoram or thyme

½ teaspoon cumin

6-ounce can tomato paste

2 cans cooked beans (any variety)

1 can chili con carne

handful of fresh cilantro, chopped, but not too fine

12 ounces tomato ketchup or to taste

3–4 tablespoons masa harina

Salt, to taste

Pepper flakes (added later, if more bite is wanted)

1 whole green pepper, diced

1 red onion, sliced thin

shredded cheese (cheddar, for example)

- Start with 1½ pounds of dry beans. Bridey doesn't mind the work, so she cooks several varieties: perhaps some pinto, some black (*frijoles negros*), some small red (*frijoles rojos pequeños*), a total equal to 1½ pounds, each to be cooked separately because they might require a different cooking time.

- In separate pots (if you're using more than one variety) soak overnight each variety of beans in cold water, according to the directions on the package.
- Drain, rinse and cover (plus two inches) with cold water, each in its own pot. Simmer gently till almost done, about 30 minutes. Ideally, all the cooking water will be absorbed.
- Remove and combine all beans in a single bowl.
- In a large pot, over a medium to low heat, brown the pound of ground beef, mashing the meat with a fork to make it grainy.
- Remove the ground beef to a plate.
- In the big pot, brown the sausage in the juices of the ground beef.
- Remove the sausage and add it to the plate with the ground beef.
- In the big pot, brown the beef chunks.
- Remove the beef and add to the plate with the ground beef and sausage.
- In the big pot, add a tablespoon of olive oil and sauté the onions until they begin to brown.
- When the onions are half-cooked, add the minced garlic.
- When onions begin to brown, sprinkle the

paprika over the garlic and onion mixture and stir well.

- Add marjoram (or thyme), black pepper and cumin.
- Stir the tomato paste into the mixture.
- Reduce the heat to low. Add all the meats and the bowl of beans, mix well and cook covered for 40 minutes, stirring occasionally to prevent sticking.
- Add the canned beans, canned chili and cilantro, and mix well.
- Continue cooking five more minutes.
- Stir in the ketchup gradually, and keep tasting as you add.
- Stir in the masa harina.
- Add red pepper flakes to taste (the amount of bite is optional).
- Continue cooking till the meat chunks are soft and the beans are cooked through, maybe 45 minutes. But keep checking.
- Add diced green pepper and sliced red onion.
- Simmer ten more minutes. Add salt to taste.
- Top with the shredded cheese, stirring the cheese lightly into the surface of the chili.
- Simmer just a minute or two, to let the cheese melt a little into the chili.

And serve—to loud acclaim!

### Swedish Beef with capers, beets and egg yolks
(Biff a la Lindström)

Parties at the Norquist home across the street always featured a magnificent smörgåsbord—a fabulous buffet array of Swedish delicacies—and Mrs. Norquist loved to have the children cook with her. Bridey and Mrs. Norquist's youngest daughter, Pia, were only four years old and already best friends, and both girls loved to cook "like grown-ups." Bridey remembers the day Mrs. Norquist pulled a couple of tall chairs over to the kitchen counter and taught the little girls how to mash and form the mixture that makes this delicious version of little Scandinavian hamburgers. Bridey felt so special, being allowed to prepare treats for the guests, and still believes this affectionate and homey environment was the beginning of her love of good cooking.

2 pounds ground beef (chuck or round, lean)
3 baking potatoes, boiled and mashed
3 egg yolks
¾ cup heavy cream or sour cream
3 pickled beets, diced
1 large onion, chopped fine
3 tablespoons capers, chopped
salt

white pepper or sweet paprika
3 tablespoons butter
Parsley sprigs

- Mix the beef and mashed potatoes thoroughly together.
- Beat the egg yolks and cream together lightly.
- Stir the egg and cream mixture gradually into the beef and potatoes till well combined.
- Add beets, onions and capers and mix well.
- Season to taste with salt and white pepper (or sweet paprika).
- Form into small, flat cakes and brown quickly in butter.
- Place on a hot platter, garnished with sprigs of parsley.

Serve with fried potatoes (Swedish style, fried with a little sugar).

***Beef Bourguignon*** (so French, so very French!)

Bridey knows that great cuisine comes from every corner of the earth, but she is convinced the French have something special. As she told Mack, you can't have good cooking without something from France. One of her dreams is to someday spend many weeks wandering all over France, learning how that "something special" is achieved. Her recipe for beef bourguignon is one version; she knows there are others.

½ pound bacon, cut in small cubes
2 teaspoons olive oil (more if needed)
3 pounds stewing beef, cut in small cubes
1 medium onion, sliced
1 clove garlic, minced
½ teaspoon salt
¼ teaspoon black pepper
2 tablespoons flour
3 cups full-bodied red wine
1 tablespoon tomato paste (optional)
¼ teaspoon marjoram
¼ teaspoon thyme
1 dried bay leaf
2 cups beef bouillon or beef stock (canned is okay)

- Preheat oven to 425°.
- In a casserole (not glass!) or Dutch oven, on the stovetop, brown the bacon lightly.
- Remove the bacon to a plate.
- Pat the beef dry with a paper towel.
- In the hot oil and bacon fat, brown the beef.
- Remove the beef to the plate with the bacon.
- Sauté onion lightly in the mixed oil and bacon fat.
- When the onion is transparent, add the garlic and continue sautéing until onion is lightly browned.
- Add all meat and mix together.
- Sprinkle salt, pepper and flour over the meat and onion and toss thoroughly.
- To coat and brown the meat, place the casserole in the oven and heat for 4 minutes.
- Remove, stir all, scrape any brown bits loose from the casserole and stir into the meat. Return to oven for 4 more minutes.
- Turn oven heat down to 325°.
- Into 3 cups of a strong red wine, stir tomato paste, ¼ teaspoon marjoram, ¼ teaspoon thyme, 1 bay leaf, mix well and pour over meat. If more liquid is needed, add beef bouillon or beef stock to just cover the meat.

- Bring to a simmer on the stovetop, then cover and return to the oven to simmer slowly 3 to 4 hours, or until beef is tender.

(Optional: flambé a small glass of cognac or brandy and add to the meat just before serving.) Serve with small buttered potatoes.

**Center Point Large Print**
600 Brooks Road / PO Box 1
Thorndike ME 04986-0001 USA

**(207) 568-3717**

**US & Canada:**
**1 800 929-9108**
www.centerpointlargeprint.com